A BALM OF HEALING

SYDNEY
WINWARD

A BALM OF HEALING

SUNLIGHT AND SHADOWS BOOK 5

This is a work of fiction. Names, characters, places, and incidents are either the product of the author's imagination or are used fictitiously, and any resemblance to actual persons living or dead, business establishments, events, or locales, is entirely coincidental.

A Balm of Healing

COPYRIGHT © 2023 Sydney Winward

Cover Design by MiblArt

Published by Silver Forge Books

All rights reserved. No part of this book may be used or reproduced in any manner whatsoever without written permission of the author except in the case of brief quotations embodied in critical articles or reviews.

Paperback ISBN 978-1-960461-03-2

Digital ISBN 978-1-960461-02-5

www.sydneywinward.com

To those who still dream of love

BOOKS BY SYDNEY
WINWARD

The Bloodborn Series
Bloodborn
Bloodbond
Bloodscourge
Bloodbane
Bloodcurse

**Sunlight and Shadows
Series**
A Breath of Sunlight
A Taste of Shadows
A Glimpse of Music
A Kiss of Embers
A Balm of Healing

Letters to Love Series
Yours, Sterling
Forever, Mirabelle
Always, Ivette

Lord Death Series
A Waltz with Lord Death

Novellas
Through Wylder Meadows
Root Brew Float
On Silver Wings
Bloodmoon
Selkie

CHAPTER ONE

ALL OF EMERIC Dalena's forty-three years' worth of pride withered away in a single moment as a knock sounded on the front door of his new home.

The nurse had arrived.

His hands clenched over the wheels of his wooden wheelchair as he gazed out the window of a somber winter morning. Thick snow rested on every inch of his yard from the trees around his property to the waist-high black metal gates acting as yet another prison in his life to the expansive grounds that had boasted a variety of plants and flowers before the most recent snowstorm had struck.

His late wife had inherited the home just before her death, and by some miracle, the deed was now his.

But the house was too big and too quiet and too lonely.

He hated his previous prison he called Attleglade. But he loathed this prison nearly as much as the last.

A despondent sigh left his lips as his gaze lowered to his maimed legs. The Attleglade council had shattered his bones as punishment for trying to visit his daughter, Nyana, in the Sun Fae city of Heulwen. That was years ago. But he had never been the same since.

"Bastien…" He murmured his son's name, the very person who had weathered all his storms with him, who had been there when he couldn't traverse the tough terrain in his chair or reach something up high. But he'd married an Ember Fae, the queen herself. And now Emeric was alone in this blasted house that felt far too unfamiliar for him to consider it a home.

The nurse knocked on the door again, shattering his melancholy thoughts into his lap. If he opened the door, there would be no pride left to save. This was it. He was waving the white flag. His life and independence were over.

Not wanting to be a burden on either his son or daughter, he heaved another sigh as he turned his chair around and maneuvered over lush carpet and past ornately carved furniture. He grumbled when the foot of his chair smacked against the small table resting against the wall, struggling to straighten himself out before he wheeled himself into the entry room and in front of the too-large mahogany door.

The first of another round of rapping sounded on the door, and he pulled it open quickly.

And frowned.

A woman stood on the other side of the threshold, hair tucked into a fur hat and spectacles over her eyes. Snowflakes gathered on her long wool coat, and a scarf hid the other half of her face to show only her eyes.

Those eyes stared back at him, nearly as wide as her spectacles as she took him in. But then the corners of her eyes crinkled with a smile.

She held out a gloved hand to him. "Sir, my name is Gweneth Caddell. I'm so pleased to meet your acquaintance!"

"Who are you?" he grumbled, taking in her smooth skin free of wrinkles and her straight posture. "Surely, you are not the nurse I recently hired."

Slowly, she lowered her hand, but the smile never left her eyes. "That's me. Nurse Caddell."

Emeric gaped at her and dug into his pocket, unfolding a piece of parchment and waving it in the air. "Your application said you were fifty-three."

She snatched the paper from him and winced. "I have a hard time with letters and numbers, sir."

"You are illiterate?"

She shook her head. "I often write them backward or out of order by accident. It was not my intention to deceive you about my age. I am thirty-five."

"Nearly twenty years younger than I anticipated," he breathed. Louder, he said, "I have no choice but to reject your application. I hope you can find employment elsewhere—"

But as he tried to close the door in her face, she planted her foot in the doorway to prevent it from closing.

"Please, sir." Her smile melted, her eyes pleading with him. "I need this job."

"I can't have a younger woman staying in this house with me."

"I won't stay," she stammered. "I have a place in the city. I can cook and clean and mend." She glanced at his legs and smacked herself in the forehead. "And I have healing magic!"

After a moment, he opened the door wider and scrutinized her. Most of her was hidden beneath wool and fur and spectacles. Of course, he already knew she was a nurse. But healing magic? Only one type of fae was capable of such a feat...

"Take off your hat."

She quickly did as he asked, and his heart caught at the beautiful brown waves cascading over her shoulders and down her back. His gaze lingered a little longer on her flat, pointed ears that marked her as a Sun Fae.

The sight of a Sun Fae punched him in the gut, stealing the air from his lungs until he couldn't breathe. The ears alone reminded him of his late wife, Meredith. And the reminder of her hurt immensely.

"I apologize." She straightened her spectacles. "I usually keep my hair pinned up. I can assure you that I maintain a professional appearance and demeanor at all times."

Obviously, he hadn't been around women in a very long time, especially those not of Forest Fae origin, because he kept staring, his tongue tied in knots. The woman was eight years younger than him and beautiful, too. He'd always fancied Sun Fae women with their long ears and bright smiles and the style of clothing they wore.

Nurse! his mind screamed, waking him from his stupor. He really should have turned her away despite her apparently desperate need for employment. But if she truly possessed healing magic... At the very least, an interview was in order.

He sighed and motioned her into the house. "I'll put on a pot of tea. Let's discuss more inside."

She followed him in, and he started to lead her forward when he stopped suddenly, unable to glance away when she shed her coat, scarf, and hat to reveal a deep plum dress with long, snug sleeves to her wrist and a hem that brushed against brown boots. A belt was cinched at her small waist, with several pouches and foreign items dangling from it. Nursing tools or medicines, perhaps?

But when she took off her spectacles to wipe the lenses, his heart faltered again when the absence of them on her face revealed almond-shaped, olive-green eyes.

He scratched his long, pointed ear with a slight droop to it to mark him as a Forest Fae and pinched the bridge of his nose as he reminded himself that his life was long over. No woman would look twice at him, and the only reason he didn't try to throw her out again was to keep what small amount of pride remained. After a short chat about her qualifications, he would send her on her way and look for someone older and plumper and with quite a few more wrinkles.

But what could one simple chat hurt? He was lonely, and she was pretty.

"You poor fool," he muttered as he wheeled himself into the expansive kitchen with her following at his wheels. A large table lay on one side of the room, and on the other was the stove, sink, and all manner of cupboards and cookware. A part of him disliked the unfamiliarity of this home with its pipes and its wall paint and its smooth floors. He'd previously lived inside a cozy tree. This place was not cozy.

He was overly aware of Gweneth's attention on him as he sparked a fire in the stove, placed a kettle filled with water on top, and tossed in his tea herbs to steep. While the water heated, he gathered two porcelain cups and placed them on either side of the table. She pulled her own chair out, and only then did he internally berate himself. When was the last time he'd been chivalrous?

Likely some fourteen-odd years ago.

When the kettle whistled, he strained the tea into the cups and locked his chair opposite her. After taking a sip of the earthy tea, he glanced up.

To find her gawking again.

"Pardon me for staring." Her cheeks filled with a rosy blush as she caught one more glimpse before lowering her gaze to her tea. "I have never seen a Forest Fae before. Your hair is so…" She glanced up and blushed again. "*White.* But you look so young."

"You've never seen a Forest Fae before? Surely, you've caught at least a glimpse of one."

The woman shook her head before nodding. "Well, I have seen plenty of forest folk. But none like *you.* Your people are the heart of the forest."

"The heart…" He released a long breath and shook his head slowly. "I don't know about that. Though, I will agree that my people have kept themselves isolated from others for many years."

Her mouth lifted in the faintest smile before she blew on the steam wafting above her cup. "Honestly, when I applied for the job, I expected… Well, I thought you might be closer to death's door than the birthing womb, if you catch my meaning."

For the first time in ages, he almost smiled. "I am a father of a twenty-two-year-old son and a twenty-four-year-old daughter. Not as close to the birthing womb as I wish I was."

"Oh." Another blush as she averted her gaze. "I didn't realize you were married."

He gazed intensely down at his amber-colored tea to avoid glancing her way. "Meredith has been gone for some time now."

"I'm so sorry to hear that…" Another pause, but to his surprise, it wasn't an awkward silence like he experienced with others when he mentioned her passing.

A longer pause followed before she met his eye once more. "May I ask your age?"

He quirked his mouth to the side as he stared across the table at her, his attention dropping to the lip she bit between her teeth before he occupied himself with a loose thread of his tunic. It was Forest Fae in nature, one of the few belongings he'd managed to take with him after he'd escaped the forest.

"Forty-three," he answered quietly.

"Oh." She smiled, disarming him entirely when she tucked a strand of hair behind her ear. "I'm thirty-five. But I suppose you already knew that, what with my mix-up on my application. Which we haven't even spoken of yet. I assure you, I am fully qualified for whatever task you place in my path. I can cook. I can clean. I can run errands. I have years of experience in the medical field. Really, you need not doubt me." She reached across the table and squeezed his arm, which rested on the table, before her eyes snapped wide open and she released him. "Oh, dear." She took a long sip of her tea, silence following in the wake of her rambling.

Emeric stared at the woman with a puzzled expression. He knew his life was over. He was maimed. He was too old to catch the attention of a beautiful young woman.

Then why did it seem like she was flirting with him?

He almost scoffed and rolled his eyes. He hadn't been on the marriage market for quite some time. He was far off his game.

"Tell me about your nursing experience." He'd already resigned himself to reject her application at the end of the interview, but asking wouldn't hurt.

"Well…" She shrugged one shoulder and gestured to herself. "I think my name speaks for itself, no?"

But he only stared at her, trying to figure out if she was jesting or serious. "I have been sequestered in the forest most of my life. I have never heard your name before."

This time, her entire face burned red, and her next sentence stammered from her mouth. "I-I-I didn't r-r-realize…" Her fingers flew to the green brooch attached to her dress at her collar, and she clasped it within her hand. "I have served as a healer under lords and kings, traveling from one kingdom to the next. One day, I hope to serve in King Calle's castle. Though, I know it's a distant dream considering he already has plenty of healers at his fingertips. But either way, I trained in my profession in Heulwen, and I've traveled the seven kingdoms for fifteen years now." Her thumb brushed the brooch in a circular motion. "I'll admit, most of my experience is healing, but I am equal to the task of cleaning and baking and mending. Truly."

He steepled his fingers together and rested his chin on top. "King Calle is my granddaughter's father."

Gweneth's lips parted as she stared at him. And stared some more. "His daughter is—"

"—Maisy Everdon."

"Then…you are like royalty."

Emeric pushed away from the table and dumped the rest of the tea into the sink. He was done with this interview. "Not quite." He gave her a regretful look. "I apologize, Miss Caddell. But I have to deny—"

His words cut off as she rounded on him with determination in her brows, and before he managed to stop her, she grasped both of his shoulders with her hands, and a burst of energy shot through his body.

He gasped as he felt her magic thread through his veins, seeking, searching. Until it traveled back the way it had come and exited him completely, leaving him breathless.

"The bones in your legs are shattered," she said matter-of-factly as she released his shoulders and faced him with a determined look in her eye. "Your hip is crooked, which likely is causing you a great deal of pain. Your muscles are withered from disuse. The blood flow to your lower extremities is low, which is likely causing other problems. I would guess you are often out of breath after short periods of using your wheelchair. Your body is weak, and—"

"What are you getting at?" he snarled, now hurrying to the entry room to usher her out of his house even faster. He grabbed her belongings and shoved them into her arms. "I think you have overstayed your welcome. Leave. Now."

Gweneth lifted her chin in defiance to his dismissal. "What I'm trying to say is your injuries are old and extensive. But I am confident I can fix them."

Ice struck him through the chest as he stared back at her with disbelief. His jaw slackened, and for a brief moment, her fervor almost made him believe… "It's impossible."

"Nothing is impossible, sir." She shrugged into her coat and pulled her hat over her head. "I will return tomorrow morning to give you more time to think about what I'm offering." She nodded her head. "Good day."

A chilly breeze entered the house in her wake, and when she closed the door behind her, several snowflakes brushed across the floor before melting quickly against the warmth inside.

For far too long, he stared at the door, overcome by shock.

A flashback of his time in the Attleglade forest pulled him into the darkness of his memories.

Branches had weaved around his wrists and ankles, securing him to the ground. He'd thrashed and screamed against his restraints, and when that hadn't worked, he'd begged the council to take Bastien away, only a boy at the time, so he didn't have to witness what was about to transpire.

But they'd held Bastien steady, forcing him to watch as they broke every bone in Emeric's legs thrice over.

He'd never known such agony could exist.

He'd never known he could hate so deeply after they had scarred his son for life with the images that would likely never leave his mind.

The pain of recovery had been brutal. And the knowledge that he'd never walk again had cut him deeply until there was nothing left to bleed.

Gweneth couldn't possibly fix his legs.

Could she?

CHAPTER TWO

Gweneth wrestled with her skirts in one hand as she trudged through ankle-deep snow while carrying a portmanteau in the other hand. The wind smashed white powder into her face, stinging what was visible of her skin and quickly fogging up her spectacles.

With a huff, she pulled the spectacles off her face and stuffed them inside her skirt pocket. The way ahead became a blur, but it was better than not being able to see anything at all.

Grumbles escaped her mouth as she followed the road leading to town. She was angry. Not just at Mr. Dalena but at herself. What was she thinking grabbing him like that to try to exploit what likely might be his greatest insecurity? And all for what? A job?

A job she desperately needed…

She frowned as she stopped for a moment to glance inside her coin purse strapped to her belt. Only a few coins remained. Enough for a couple more meals, but it would hardly pay for a room to shelter her from the elements.

She'd never been so poor in her life. Mr. Dalena had been her last hope for a roof over her head. At least until she could get back on her feet.

But she had seen the immediate dismissal in his eyes, and she'd done what she had to do to survive.

Had it been a mistake?

"It's because of my age, isn't it?" She kicked a plume of snow with her boot but immediately regretted it when it whipped up and somehow found its way down her blouse. She gritted her teeth and continued her tromping through the snow. "To be clear," she continued talking to herself, "I had no idea you lived alone, and I definitely didn't realize you were young and *handsome!*"

Another kick. This time, she gasped as she kicked ice rather than powder, wincing as pain flared up her foot.

She focused her magic downward until a pleasant coolness enveloped her foot. After a few moments, the pain subsided, and the throbbing ceased. When she placed weight on it and it didn't hurt, she continued into town.

Children laughed and ran around the streets. Carts pulled by horses creaked by, giving her little choice but to hug the brick walls of the buildings as they passed. Humans and fae alike went about their day, even in the cold temperatures, recognizable by their ears alone—if they were visible. Humans had round ears. Sun Fae, like herself, had long ears flat against their heads. Several brown-haired Forest Fae sported ears with a bit of a droop, while Water Fae had rounded ears in their human forms and webbed ears in their merpeople forms.

She spotted one Shadow Fae haggling wares across the square, his short, pointed ears visible beneath the black curls shaping his head. His eyes appeared haggard as if he had no desire to be awake during daylight hours. Those types of fae were nocturnal, the most mysterious and albeit dangerous fae of all.

Anxious exhaustion weighed on her own shoulders, and she slumped onto a wooden barrel hidden in the corner of the square, head in her hands. In her current…situation…the only way she could get through winter was to find live-in positions in someone's home, or trade healing work for a place to rest her head. Mr. Dalena had been the only one in Ebriel seeking such a person, but now she'd gone and squandered her opportunity.

"Now what?" she murmured to herself.

The farther she traveled from Heulwen, the more likely she was to find work, especially given her High Healer status. But she hadn't enough for a wagon fare, and she couldn't possibly travel to the next town by herself on foot in the middle of winter.

"It's all right," she told herself as she lifted her head from her hands. "This is just a minor setback. All I need to do is get through winter. Find an odd job here and there. Locate a place to rent."

With renewed determination, she weaved through the growing crowds and started down the street leading toward the nearest inn. Two male and one female Sun Fae leaned against the railing, watching her as she ascended the steps. She winced at the racket her portmanteau made as it banged against the stairs, and once more as it hit the corner of the door frame on her way inside.

A hum of voices greeted her, along with the sweet scent of morning porridge. Her stomach protested against its emptiness, but she silently told it to hush. There was no sense in drawing more attention to herself than necessary.

"Pardon me," she said as she approached the counter, waving down the woman pouring several bowls of porridge. "Do you have any empty rooms?"

The woman shook her head apologetically. "The winter solstice is a few days away. The Shadow folk have come crawling out of their caves—" A Shadow Fae sitting at one of the tables lifted his head and glared, and the innkeeper grimaced. "I mean to say that most of our rooms are occupied by Shadow Fae."

Gweneth placed her palms face up on the counter between them. "I am a healer looking for work. I will trade services for a room and a few meals."

The other woman clicked her tongue. "There is no need for your services here. Have you tried The Healer's Cottage?"

She nodded. "There are no healing positions available."

And then the woman pointed north. "A handicapped man just moved in about a month ago in Northcott's old place. Rumor is he's looking for a nurse."

A groan escaped her mouth as she dropped her forehead on the counter with a resounding *thump*. The wooden slab muffled her voice as she asked, "Is there anyone else looking for help? Anyone at all?" At this point, she would take any work even if it wasn't in her usual profession.

Holding up a finger, the woman disappeared for a moment before returning with several advertisements and placing them on the counter in front of her. "I know this isn't quite what you are looking for, but these positions have been available for a while."

Gweneth sifted through the papers, her grimace growing with each surveyed job.

Rat catcher.

Beast hunter.

Chimney sweep.

Waste management.

"I am a High Healer, for shadow's sake!" she exclaimed. "These jobs are beneath me and out of my skill set."

The woman gave her a sympathetic look as she picked up the bowls of porridge. "It depends on how desperate you are for a wage." And then she shuffled away to wait on her guests.

She returned her attention to the flier and brushed her thumb along her brooch, the last thing she had of her mother. The only thing she hadn't sold…

She pushed the melancholy aside and focused on her predicament. She hadn't the faintest idea how to catch rats. She'd sooner get killed than hunt down a beast. A chimney sweep? Perhaps she might be able to accomplish that, but during the winter it would be a miserable job. And she wanted to bury her head and pretend she hadn't seen the waste management advertisement.

"There has to be something else I can do," she said to herself before pushing the advertisements away and braving the chilly winter air once more.

For the next several hours, she darkened the doors of businesses, the orphanage, and she wrestled with the idea of visiting people's homes. But as the afternoon transitioned to evening and she barely afforded to fill her belly with cheese and a loaf of bread, she firmed her resolve and began knocking on doors.

Many didn't answer. Others quickly turned her away.

And then she found herself back in the market square, the area much less crowded than it had been during the afternoon. She rubbed her hands up and down her arms, her fingers and toes frozen, along with her nose and ears.

"I am a High Healer," she whispered, her breath escaping as a cloud of fog. "This isn't supposed to happen to me."

Yet, she stared into her coin purse only to find it empty, save for a single coin that might buy her an apple but nothing more. A few dresses lay within her portmanteau, along with several other personal items. But no blanket or pillow. Nothing else to keep her warm.

"This isn't supposed to happen to me," she stated again as disbelief snapped its jaws around her neck. The sky darkened further by the minute until only a few lone lanterns from the outdoor stalls lit up the square.

For the first time in her entire life, she had no place warm to rest her head, no money in her purse, and nowhere to call home.

Fear jumped up her legs and crawled through her body, leaving gooseflesh in its wake. Never in her life had she worried where her next meal might come from or if she might wake up in the morning. But the chill of uncertainty wracked her entire body with shivers.

"I can do this," she murmured to herself. Though, believing her words seemed impossible.

With a heavy heart, she unclasped the brooch from her dress and approached one of the booths packing up their wares for the night—likely a trapper judging by the fur hats, boots, coats, and…blankets.

"Please." She held out her hands, offering the man her brooch. "I will trade this for a blanket. I have no other money."

Could she have traded it into a jeweler for money instead? Of course. But she didn't know where to find one within the city, and her body felt like it might collapse with weariness.

The trapper plucked the brooch from her hands and inspected it close to his face. With only a grunt, he pocketed the piece of jewelry, handed her a fur blanket, and loaded the rest of his wares into a cart pulled by a horse.

Gweneth held the blanket close to her chest as she roamed the dark streets, her gaze darting back and forth across her path as if someone might jump out of the shadows and grab her. She searched for a barn to sneak into or an awning to shelter her from the elements. All she found were two brick walls of an empty alleyway blocking out the snow drifting from the skies.

"Just one night," she promised herself as she took out one of her dresses and laid it on the ground to protect her from the chill of the street. She lay on top, shivering uncontrollably as she pulled the fur blanket over herself. The setup wasn't ideal, but homeless people managed to survive on the streets all the time. Surely, she could survive just one night.

Just one night...

CHAPTER THREE

"RIDICULOUS GLOVES!" Emeric grumbled to himself as he wheeled his chair down the street *outside* in the middle of the blistering winter. He'd waited all morning for Miss Caddell to arrive. And when she hadn't, he resorted to outfitting himself in warm clothing and braving the elements in only his wheelchair with no help whatsoever.

His wooden wheels slid across patches of ice. His gloves slipped repeatedly, making maneuvering the blasted thing difficult. Mounds of snow on the path ahead of him caused him to use far too much effort to roll over each obstacle. By the time he reached the town square, he found himself out of breath and ready to collapse from exhaustion.

Usually, his son, Bastien, would maneuver him over such obstacles. But now that he lived as the Ember Queen's husband within the forest, Emeric was without a strong pair of arms to help him seemingly with little effort.

A pit of sadness welled within his chest at the thought of Bastien. He missed him. Far too much. He didn't know how to live without his son, his previous constant companion. He felt…lost. As if he was a puppet and someone else commanded the strings.

People stared at him as he passed, speaking in hushed voices to one another. Not many people lived their lives in a wheelchair, and he imagined it was a shocking sight.

But if there was even the slightest chance of ridding himself of his wheelchair altogether, he was willing to take it.

However, he hadn't the slightest idea of where to find Miss Caddell. Had she left the city?

Emeric asked around the square, trying to find out if anyone had seen her. Several people vaguely remembered speaking to her yesterday. Others couldn't recall her name or face.

He nearly turned around and started in another direction when he caught sight of a familiar green brooch pinned to a woman's blouse, with a silver, decorative edge around the shiny oval pendant.

"Where did you get that?" he asked the woman, who sat on a crate while her husband sold wares to several customers.

The woman regarded him cautiously. "It was a gift from my husband. He gave it to me yesterday."

He ran a hand over his face and pinched the bridge of his nose. Miss Caddell had seemed overly fond of the piece of jewelry during their interview. Why would she sell it?

Begrudgingly, he dug into his pocket and pulled out his money purse. "I'll buy it from you. Is this enough?"

Instead of rejecting his proposal outright, the woman slinked closer and studied the amount offered. She quickly traded the brooch for the money, and he pocketed the jewelry inside his coat.

The woman said, "The healer traded it for a blanket. Nothing more."

For a moment, he puzzled over the new information as he left the stalls quickly lest she change her mind. A blanket? Surely, the brooch could get her more than a simple blanket. Why did she—?

The blood drained from his face as he connected the missing pieces. "Oh no."

Miss Caddell had been desperate for the job because she had nowhere else to stay. He reckoned she'd slept outside somewhere. But where?

"Where are you?" he murmured as he continued on his way down another path, dodging people, carts, and small animals as he searched for a woman with brown hair and olive-green eyes. If he were in her position, he'd find a barn to sleep in. But where were barns located within the city?

His gaze darted about, his fingers growing colder the longer he spent outside. But he refused to give up his search. And when he spotted the silhouette of a barn in the distance, he started toward it while continuing to scan the area around him.

But when he glanced down an alleyway, he froze when he spotted a lump lying on the ground, covered in a fur blanket.

He turned his chair at a sharp angle, the wheels sliding across a patch of ice and nearly making him crash before he managed to gain control of it once more. Beneath the blanket lay a huddled figure, unmoving.

Panic jumped through his chest when he recognized the brunette locks, the long, dark eyelashes, the purple of her dress. Gweneth lay still, frost gathered on her lashes and coat.

Not able to reach her with his arms, he snatched a loose, wooden board leaning against the wall and prodded her in the side.

No response.

"Wake up!" he cried, prodding her hard enough in the stomach for her to emit an "Oof!"

Gweneth bolted upright and glanced blearily at their surroundings before her gaze landed on him. She squinted up at him, and he knew he should have said something, but his heart still ricocheted through his veins, even as relief tried to calm his erratic pulse.

Finally, his tongue worked enough for him to speak. "You said you had a place to stay in town."

"Blazing crickets," she croaked under her breath as she scrambled for the spectacles she pulled from her pocket. After placing them over her nose, she ducked her head and blushed, her words having trouble escaping as if her throat and mouth were frozen. "If I'm honest, I had no plan other than to accept the job you extended to me. All the rooms at the inn are full. And…" She rubbed her hands up and down her arms. "I had nowhere else to go."

Emeric inhaled a long breath and released it slowly before he wheeled himself around and started toward the alley's exit. He stopped several paces away and glanced back at her. "Well? Are you coming or not?"

The woman inhaled sharply, her eyes wide before she hastily packed her portmanteau and stumbled after him. "Does this mean you are offering me the job after all?"

"It's temporary," he clarified, avoiding eye contact. Mother Autumn knew housing a beautiful woman was not going to be easy. "I can't have you sleeping outside in the snow. You hear?"

From the corner of his eye, he noticed her nodding enthusiastically. "I will be the best caretaker, housekeeper, and healer you've ever had. Mark my words." She paused behind him, but his arms continued forcing his damp, snowy wheels through the infuriating obstacles. "Do you need me to push—"

"No," he growled. "The answer is always no. I can do it myself."

"Ah." She moved into step beside him instead. "That's good to know, because you look heavy, and I don't want the added strain."

Her jest lifted his brows in surprise, and he found himself staring at her twitching mouth, her lips nearly blue from freezing herself overnight. Her face was pale, and he didn't miss her shivering limbs even as she struggled to keep up with him as if her legs didn't work properly.

When they reached the short black gate of his home, Miss Caddell appeared as if she might collapse at any moment, and he didn't think he was in any shape to catch her.

He ushered her up the ramp leading to his front door, and when they entered the structure, he urged her to sit on the sofa in the main room while he proceeded to drape several warm blankets over her shoulders. He disappeared into the kitchen only for a few minutes before he brought back a tray of food and tea, carefully balanced on his lap.

Her eyes widened as he set it on the table in front of her.

"I'm supposed to take care of *you*," she protested, teeth chattering.

"And you can't do so without the use of your limbs. I suggest you take some time to rest and warm up before you do any sort of work around the house."

She gazed back at him with parted lips, and he couldn't help but return her stare. A foreign flutter took hold of his stomach, tying it and twisting it until he wasn't sure whether he would retch or flee from nerves. He felt like a young man again, entranced as he laid eyes on a beautiful, captivating woman.

But then the curtain fell over him as he reminded himself he was worthless. It would do him good to remind himself often.

"Did you come find me?" she asked, halting him in the tracks of his retreat.

He nodded once. "You said you would show up today. You never came."

"Because you want to know if I can heal you."

There was no sense in denying it. He nodded again. "I hate my life," he confessed as he stared at his hands resting in his lap. "It's sad and lonely and filled with so much heartache and pain. But I thought if I just had the slightest bit of use in my legs…maybe that could change things."

"What happened?" she asked quietly. "I've seen more injuries than you can count. And I've never seen anything like yours."

The aching pit of sadness returned with a vengeance as he recalled everything he'd lost. Not just his wife. But his legs. His magic. His independence. His identity. But if she were to help him, she needed to know the truth.

"Where I used to live, the council was cruel. I…" He cleared his throat and stared at his hands just to keep himself from glancing her way. "I was the chief's heir at the time. But it was just a title." He ran a hand through his white hair, now curled at his ears without a haircut for a while. "I escaped

Attleglade and married Meredith. After eleven years when my father died, they found me. Us. Threatened to kill my family if I didn't return to do the chief's job." He swallowed, his eyes smarting with emotion, enough that he turned his chair to face away from her. "She took Nyana. I took Bastien. Soon after, Meredith died." He rubbed a hand over his chest as he relived memories he wished he could bury. "I tried to visit Nyana in secret. I got caught. My punishment was to never walk again." He paused for several long moments to compose himself before he dared to meet her eye, only to find compassion in their depths. "I don't believe such healing is possible, Miss Caddell. But if you would be willing to try, I will pay you for your efforts."

She abandoned her place on the sofa and approached, resting a gentle hand on his shoulder. "I won't lie to you. Healing from such injuries will be painful. Perhaps just as painful as it was to receive them. Are you sure you want to proceed?"

Without hesitation, he nodded. "I would do anything to chase my grandchildren around the yard and move around independently."

The small squeeze she gave his shoulder also squeezed his heart with surprising warmth. "Give me the rest of the day to prepare, and we can begin tomorrow."

He wagged his finger at her accusingly. "You are just trying to stay here for as long as possible."

But then his heart jolted when she laughed, a beautiful, musical sound that left him both speechless and unable to form a coherent thought. Throughout his life, he'd had very little laughter to fill the gaps of heartache. But she offered hers so freely to him.

The woman's eyes sparkled with humor as she dropped her hand from his shoulder and picked up her portmanteau. "Believe me, Mr. Dalena. You don't want a healer with frozen hands."

"You may call me Emeric," he finally managed through a hoarse croak.

With a warm smile, she replied, "Then you may call me Gwen. Is there a room I can stay in for the time being?"

The main room resided on the ground floor, which was where he stayed because he couldn't climb the stairs. But the others... "All of the rooms are upstairs." He grimaced. "I apologize. I don't know how clean the second floor is. But my daughter, Nyana, assured me there are extra linens in the hall closet."

She paused on the first step leading to the next story and turned back to face him. "May I ask a personal question?"

"I suppose."

"Why don't you stay with family?"

He dropped his gaze to his lap. "Bastien recently married. He has been my rock for years. But I knew it was time to let him go on his own. And Nyana... She has three children to care for. She doesn't need me in her life. Especially because I hardly know her."

"Right," she murmured. "Meredith took Nyana. I'm sure developing a new relationship with your daughter is not easy."

Not knowing how to reply, he remained quiet. He'd never confessed the inner ponderings of his mind, the workings of his heart on such a level before with someone he just met.

"First thing tomorrow," she said as she continued her trek up the stairs. "Make sure you are ready."

In all honesty, he never thought he could be ready for what he might face.

CHAPTER FOUR

"WHAT DOES A High Healer do, exactly, as opposed to a normal healer?" Emeric asked from where he watched her dig into her portmanteau. The man sat on his bed, legs dangling over the edge, as he wore an expression of deep vulnerability.

Time and again, Gweneth had witnessed such vulnerability in her patients. A hesitance to trust. An uncertainty of what was to come. An insecurity about their physical and mental shortcomings. But she tried her best to reassure them even if with only a gentle touch or quiet word.

She pulled out her fingerless healer gloves and slipped them on either hand. The soft leather formed perfectly over her fingers, and the magic infused inside the golden sun stones on each knuckle helped channel the intensity of her magic.

"A High Healer is someone who has trained more extensively in the healing arts. Think of it as a comparison between an apprentice and a master in a trade."

"Then you are a master at your craft."

She offered a smile, which immediately melted the uncertainty in his expression and replaced it with obvious fluster. She enjoyed the way his Forest Fae ears turned a slight shade of pink, a stark contrast to the white of his hair.

"Most women don't reach the High Healer status, as they often drop their trade in favor of having children and keeping a house. I'll admit I have pushed away such distractions to focus on my career."

Emeric scratched his pink ear. "Then you are unmarried. No children?"

With a shake of her head, she pushed an armchair closer to the bed and sat within its soft, red- and gold-patterned cushions. The rest of the room was similar in its ornate design. Thick drapes cascaded from black curtain rods on either side of the window. Two bedside tables and a writing desk lay against the walls with fancy handles and intricate knobs. A vast rug lay beneath the bed, cushioning her stockinged feet with far more luxury than she had ever experienced.

However, even amidst the fine things around her, she got the distinct impression that Emeric was uncomfortable in his own home. This was not his own place of comfort. And like he had mentioned the day before, he was not happy here.

"Will you allow me to touch your legs?" she asked, seeking permission first this time.

Despite his previous eagerness for the chance at healed legs, he hesitated. Uncertainty returned once again, and dare she think it, a bit of self-consciousness.

She tried to offer reassurance. "You are not the first wheelchair-bound person I have seen to. I can imagine your muscles have atrophied due to you being unable to use them. I also assume your bones healed incorrectly, causing you disjointed or even chronic pain."

Without a word, he nodded his permission, and she reached down and carefully picked up his feet and placed them on her lap. He winced but otherwise offered no indication of further pain.

Slowly, she peeled off his socks and pushed his trousers up to his knees. Usually, she regarded injuries like this with a professional air about her. But knowing how he received them churned her stomach with horror.

His feet were locked in unnatural positions. The bones in his legs were twisted and jutted out at terrible angles beneath the skin.

"I'm glad you escaped from that place," was all she managed to say in the face of her wavering emotions.

A shuddering breath escaped his mouth. "Bastien's friend, Ashryn, is now the chief of the village. Attleglade has changed for the better. But I still can't bring myself to return. Everyone there thinks I died in a fire. I'd prefer to keep it that way."

"I will take your secret to my grave."

She reached out with her magic, allowing it to flow through his body to get an exact idea of the extent of the damage. It was any wonder he thought healing his legs was impossible. Bones were shattered and crooked and healed completely wrong.

Finally, her magic retreated, and her lips pressed tightly together as she glanced up to meet his eye. "To give you back the use of your legs, I am going to have to rebreak every single bone in an extremely precise way before they can heal again."

"So it's impossible," he sighed.

"No." She shook her head and unsuccessfully held back a grin. "It's not impossible. It's *time consuming*. This type of surgery will take me hours upon hours. I may have to do it in two or three sessions to give myself a few breaks. But it will be painful for you."

His jaw dropped as he stared back at her with disbelief in his eyes. She gently set his legs back down before pulling out a small briefcase from her portmanteau and opened it to reveal three rows of elixirs within glass vials.

Not giving him a chance to answer in his shock, she held up a vial with amber liquid and thoroughly shook it up. "I would like to keep you unconscious to prevent you from feeling the worst of the pain. And I possess such medicine to take away the bite of the healing process." She stopped in front of him and momentarily ceased shaking the vial. "Emeric, do you still want to continue?"

He ran his fingers through his hair, and a sudden desire to do the same surfaced unexpectedly. Of course, she had healed many different men of different races. Plenty of them were handsome. But something about Emeric gave her heart pause. His attractiveness. His calm soul. His vulnerability. His fragile hope.

I can't afford to get distracted, she reminded herself. Her career mattered more than a handsome face. Besides, a relationship would only hold her back from achieving her dreams.

"I would be a fool to decline," he replied. Wariness stared back at her through his small window of hope. "You've done this sort of thing before?"

"Yes." She instructed him to lay back on the bed. In any ordinary circumstance, she would prefer to work with her patient on a cot somewhere other than their personal rooms. But Emeric's mobility was limited. "Never to this great extent. But I have corrected poorly healed breaks plenty of times."

"How much will this cost me?"

She paused as she took him in, followed by the lavish decorations surrounding them. It would be easy to take advantage of the man, who clearly had plenty of money to spend. She had suddenly found herself dirt poor, after all. But doing such a thing was out of character for her. No matter how desperate she was.

"I only want one thing from you."

"Anything."

She inhaled a long breath and let it out slowly. "If my performance is satisfactory, perhaps you might write me a letter of recommendation to the Sun King. Or at the very least, give a good word to your daughter. I really, truly want a job at the palace."

"I don't know how much my word is worth..."

"This is the closest I've ever come to reaching my dreams, Emeric. I will take whatever you will give me."

Hope flared within her chest as she held her breath, waiting for his answer. To her delight, he nodded in agreement.

"Swallow this," she instructed as she held the vial to his lips. "You will be unconscious within minutes, and then I will begin."

But instead of taking the vial from her, he caught onto her hand. Her stomach flipped at the warm, pleasant contact, especially as she gazed back into eyes as silver as a full moon.

"Please," he rasped.

She wasn't sure whether it was a plea for her to heal him, to be careful with him, to take care of his trust, or gently handle his legs. But she found herself returning the gesture with a squeeze to his fingers.

"I promise."

And then he drank the elixir.

"You are a brave man." Gweneth squeezed his hand like she did with all her patients. But with Emeric... It felt different.

No man had ever managed to spread fire through her fingers, up her arm, and engulf her entire chest in flames.

"I am a coward." His eyes drooped and snapped back open. "I never fought back when I could have. When I should have."

"Why?" she murmured as his eyelids drooped again.

"Because Bastien means more to me than anything in the world."

"You never fought back because you were protecting someone you loved." She squeezed his hand again. "That's one of the bravest things you could have done."

Twin trails of silver tears rolled down his cheeks as his eyes closed entirely. "I don't know what to do." His voice slurred. "I am nothing without my legs. Without my magic."

She started at the realization that he'd at one point possessed an affinity for magic. To lose so much after such a hefty sacrifice? Emeric deserved a happy life more than anyone she'd ever known. "Those things do not define your worth. You are a wonderful man just because of what's in here."

She touched her other hand to his chest, and she started once again when her fingers brushed against solid muscle beneath the confines of his tunic. True, many people in wheelchairs had muscular arms or torso. But he hid it so well…

Heat flared in her cheeks as she retracted her hand. Several more tears escaped his eyes before his breathing deepened, and his hand fell limp within hers. For several long moments, she held it, enjoying the simple warmth he offered, not wanting to release the pleasant but foreign emotions swirling within her chest.

But she forced herself to drop his hand and moved to stand at the foot of the bed, nearest his legs. She took a hold of each of his ankles on his left foot, closed her eyes, and channeled her magic in his foot first.

Breaking so many bones within such a short time would put a lot of stress on his body. However, the elixir would take much of the burden for him. At least during this phase.

With her magic, she felt along the broken bones nearest her hands, sensing each corner and groove where the bones had healed incorrectly.

Taking a deep breath and honing her concentration, she snapped his first bone with her magic.

The corners of his eyes winced, but he otherwise made no indication of feeling the pain.

One by one, she snapped his bones, taking care each time to place her magic correctly. No mistakes. Not for Emeric.

And when he whimpered in his sleep halfway through the surgery, still on his left leg, she administered a little more medicine to help numb the pain. Weariness tugged on her shoulders. Her belly ached from hunger. Her fingers felt stiff from holding them in the same position for so long.

She allowed herself a short break to eat from the pantry Emeric now shared with her and to flex her fingers until they felt loose and limber. And then she continued her administration until every single previously shattered piece of bone in his leg was broken.

The easy part was done. At least for this leg.

Next, she opened one of the pouches at her belt and unwrapped a cloth from a glass vial. A blinding light filled every inch of the room, and she forced herself to look away lest the bottle of sunlight damage her eyes.

She unlatched the lid from the bottle and allowed the sunlight to wash over her to invigorate her senses and fill her well of magic once more before she hid it in the confines of her belt again.

A bottle of sunlight was extremely expensive, as sunlight restored a Sun Fae's magic. She took care to keep it hidden, even when she was deep in the throes of a surgery.

With her magic restored, she allowed it to flow steadily into Emeric's leg. Little by little, she fit the bones back into place as if he was a difficult puzzle, and the wrong piece would destroy the final picture altogether.

Hours passed until the afternoon transitioned into evening, and darkness fell upon the room like a still hush. Her magic moved the final pieces of his upper thigh together before she collapsed with her elbows bracing herself against the bed near his feet.

She breathed heavily from the exertion of exhausting her magic. No strength remained to give him anymore, nor to start on the next leg. The bones were now welded together with strong sun magic, but it would still be some time before he could use his leg, especially considering the lack of strength in his muscles.

Emeric gasped suddenly as he shot upright. Heavy breaths filled his lungs, his eyes wild, and his expression contorted in pain.

"Shh, shh, shh," she soothed as she pushed him back onto the bed and ran her fingers through his hair. The texture surprised her, nearly causing her to retract her hand. His hair was soft, but also strong and thick, not at all like the white hair older people of her own race had on their heads. But the strong resilience of someone in their prime.

A whimper left his mouth, followed by a choked sob. "It hurts so much."

"I know. I know." She pulled up a chair beside the bed and held his hand while continuing to stroke his hair. "I'm only finished with one leg, I'm afraid. The extent of the damage was astronomical."

He inhaled sharply, his entire body freezing as his attention shifted toward his legs. She followed his gaze and found him slowly moving his left leg back and forth the slightest bit, regarding it as if it were an unfamiliar object not a part of him.

A wince of excruciation settled on his face, but she didn't get the chance to witness anything more when he wrapped an arm around her shoulders and pulled her into an embrace. Her heart caught at the way his sturdy arms held her, at how his steady heart beat against her ear, at the way his thumb caressed her shoulder as if she were more than a simple acquaintance.

Focus! she reminded herself, but she found it difficult when his warmth seeped into every place their bodies touched.

"I owe you the moon," Emeric said in a husky tone as he released her. "I will write you a hundred letters of recommendation if I must."

"I'm not even done yet," she laughed, shaking her head exhaustedly. "I must warn you that recovery will take much longer than a few days." She tapped a finger to her lips. "Until the end of winter, at least."

Emeric burst into laughter, shocking her into a stupor at the unfamiliar sound, at the foreign way his lips curved upward in a smile rather than a frown. For a while, she hadn't thought him capable of smiling.

"I am not going to toss you out after the surgery is complete." Perspiration beaded on his forehead, and she quickly dabbed it away with a handkerchief. "Please. Stay. As long as you need to."

"But I am a woman younger than you. I thought you had *rules* about me staying in the same house as you."

His teeth clenched as if he fought off another wave of pain. "Forget the rules," he grunted. "This is still only temporary, after all."

She sat back suddenly as the shock of heartache hit her in the chest like a hammer striking a nail. Although she'd only known Emeric for a few days, the thought of leaving churned her stomach with nausea.

What is wrong with me?

"Allow me to make you supper," she said as she stood and strode toward the doorway to put as much distance between them as possible. "Only something light on the stomach for the next several days; otherwise, I promise you won't keep it down."

Not giving him a chance to reply, she nearly sprinted out of the room and rushed into the kitchen until she found herself breathing heavily with her back pressed against the wall. She focused on steadying her breaths until her heart calmed a fraction.

Something about Emeric knocked her off balance.

And she knew it was better to leave sooner rather than later. Her career came first and foremost before anything or anyone. And no one, not even a handsome Forest Fae, would slow her down.

CHAPTER FIVE

AGONIZING HOURS PASSED painfully slowly as Emeric flitted in and out of sleep. Fire burned his left leg, and then his right as Gweneth worked on that next. The flames only grew each time he woke, the pain intensifying with every torturous hour that passed.

Thoughts of Bastien kept him grounded. His desire to move about freely and chase his grandchildren around the yard gave him the courage he needed to face the rest of the surgery.

He didn't know how much time had passed. Perhaps hours. Maybe days. But the agony faded in and out each time Gweneth's medicine blessed him with the peacefulness of slumber.

During the dark hours of night, the pain drenched him in his own perspiration. He threw off his shirt and tried to escape the confines of his blanket as he tossed back and forth, only for drowsiness to latch onto him and drag him underneath unforgiving waves. He transitioned between the sweats and the chills while fighting against the terrible pain consuming his legs.

When he woke again, the light of morning seeped through the window and lit up the entire bedroom. He blinked sluggishly, fighting against the heaviness in his head as he tried to make sense of his disorienting surroundings.

He lay beneath several thick blankets he didn't remember placing there before. A soft pillow cushioned his head, with several more pillows resting beneath his legs. Pain still coursed through them, but it was more of an intense ache rather than a fiery agony.

He stared at the ceiling for far too long as he tried to gather the courage to attempt to move his legs. If he was unable to, he feared the crushing disappointment. But if he managed the feat...

Taking a deep breath, he curled his toes. On both feet. At the same time.

Emotion caught in his throat, his eyes misting over with happiness. When was the last time he could move his legs at all, let alone his toes?

Something bright caught his attention from the corner of his eye, and he turned his head to find a waterless vase filled with a bouquet of pink and white paper flowers. His lips parted in surprise at the crisp folds and the skillful talent, and his heart warmed when he realized who they were from.

Gwen...

Where was his chair?

He located it near the foot of the bed, and he frowned at just how far away it was from his immediate grasp. Perhaps he should have continued to lay in bed, but he couldn't bear staying still for too long, even if only half of his body worked.

Gritting his teeth, he braced against the pain flaring up his legs as he attempted to maneuver himself closer to his chair. His feet protested. His legs screamed. Even his hip cautioned against the movement.

When the feat proved too difficult, he gave up and tried to lay back down on the bed but missed his mark. His body slipped off the edge, and with the foreignness of feeling, of movement in his lower extremities, he was taken off guard by the unfamiliar sensation and ended up crashing to the floor, unable to catch himself properly.

The vase tumbled after him, and although the glass didn't break, the paper flowers spilled all over his body and onto the floor beside him.

He groaned, and moments later, Gweneth rushed into the room, eyes glancing about until they rested on him where he pushed himself to sitting on the floor. Pink tinged her cheeks when she glanced from his eyes to his bare torso, her gaze lingering for several seconds. A part of him felt embarrassed for getting caught without a shirt. Another part of him felt relieved that he'd kept up with his exercises to make sure his top half remained strong even when his lower half withered in weakness.

"Did you try to walk?" she asked in a tight tone as she knelt beside him and straightened his legs out in front of him.

He shook his head. "I tried to reach my chair."

"It isn't near you for a reason, Emeric. You are not quite ready to move about."

"I can't keep lying in bed. It's agonizing."

"Because of the pain?" Her hands gently felt up his leg as if looking for broken bones or damage from the fall.

"Well, that, too. But staying down is torture. I need to be up and about. I need to be moving."

Gweneth's mouth turned upward as she released a breathy laugh. "Kin spirits, you and I. I've never really had a home. I enjoy traveling too much, going from one adventure to the next."

A spark of pain shot up his leg when she touched his knee, but a cooling relief soon chased away the discomfort as her magic flitted through the pained area. "I envy you. Life has not afforded me such adventure."

"You want to travel?"

"I've always wanted to explore the world. There has to be more out there than forest and more forest."

Her hands paused on his leg as she glanced up and met his eye. For a moment, his nostrils flared as he caught her flowery scent, and he swallowed when he realized he enjoyed it quite a bit.

When her gaze dipped again to his chest, a sense of satisfaction burned through him. Although he hadn't been on the marriage market in a very long time, he thrilled in the recognition that she felt at least a degree of attraction for him as he did for her.

"You wouldn't mind if you had to move a lot?" she asked almost distractedly as she returned her administrations to his legs. "Wouldn't you want a permanent home? What about your family?"

True, if he traveled—hypothetically—then seeing Bastien, Nyana, or his grandchildren would be more difficult. But... "I love my family. But if I got the chance to live my life, I would take it in a heartbeat."

The sweet floral aroma wafting off her skin moved closer as her touch shifted to his upper thighs. He clenched his fists where they rested against the plush rug beneath him to keep from reaching out to her.

"What do you do, Emeric?" she asked, glancing briefly at him and returning her attention to his legs. "Or, what did you do as the chieftain? I've never asked you before."

"I tried to save as many lives as possible." He frowned as he recalled with perfect clarity all of the lives he had not been able to save. Some were only children. "The council often outvoted me. But I did my best to help my people."

A breath trembled from his lungs as she placed her hands on his hips before nodding and placing the paper flowers back into the vase. "They were lucky to have you. From what it seems, you did a lot of good."

"I'm also good with my hands," he blurted but inwardly cringed, silently berating himself for his large gap in courting experience. To rectify his words, he said, "I'm a bone carver. I make tools and instruments and other trinkets. If I ever get the chance, I would sell my wares across the seven kingdoms."

The smile she gave him warmed his insides until he feared he might be catching another fever—the fever of infatuation.

"I would like to see your carvings."

She started to stand, but he grasped her elbow to keep her by his side. For just one more moment. "I've told you nearly my entire life's history. Just tell me one thing. If you can do *this*," he gestured to his legs, "then why in autumn's glory are you sleeping in alleyways in the middle of winter?"

A long sigh escaped her as she stood and placed the vase back onto the bedside table. "My mother died when I was young, and my father...he turned to gambling and drinking and more gambling. He was...unkind."

Abusive, her expression said instead as she winced.

She continued, "At the first opportunity, I left home to study the art of healing, and I never looked back. At least until I learned of my father's death and a debt collector came to...collect."

"Autumns..." he murmured, guessing the rest.

"I sold his house, all his belongings, many of mine, too. But I was left with very little in the end." Her gaze became far away as if she were somewhere other than the present. "All of my years of hard work, and all it accounted for was taking on my father's blasted debt." She winced. "Forgive me for my language."

"Believe me, I've heard far worse from Bastien." He chuckled but then quickly sobered. "I feel awful for turning you away when we met. If I had known…"

"It's all right," she reassured. "The massive debt knocked me down a peg, but this is only temporary before I get another job and get back on my feet." She stood behind him and placed her arms beneath his armpits. "On the count of three, I'm going to lift you back onto the bed. Ready?"

"No." But he gritted his teeth and braced himself as she counted down, and in a single, strong heave, she maneuvered him to the bed and helped him sit back against the pillows. "Surely, this isn't necessary."

"Just a couple more days," she promised. "Then we can begin strengthening your muscles."

He swallowed, not daring to hope but hoping anyway. "For what?"

She smiled and squeezed his hand. "For walking, Emeric. You are going to walk again."

Chapter Six

Torture. Frustration. Discouragement. But overall, hope.

Emeric received Gweneth's help with strengthening his legs over the next several weeks, first while lying on the bed, and then from his chair. And although his frustration vexed him with how weak his legs were, he knew this would take some time.

He only wished it didn't have to take so long. Gweneth could heal his bones. But she couldn't use her magic to build his muscles.

A grunt escaped his mouth as he rested both feet against the wall from where he sat in his chair. Gweneth held the chair from behind, putting weight against him, which he fought hard to resist with his shaking legs.

"Autumn's glory, woman!" he cried. "You are putting me through hell and back."

She chuckled somewhere near his ear but continued to hold the chair steady. "Just one more, Em."

"You said that five wall squats ago."

His legs shook more as he put all of his lower strength into his legs, and with one final push, he managed to straighten both legs before they collapsed from the wall and hit the ground with a thud.

Heavy breaths of exertion escaped him as he leaned back in the chair to rest after the laborious exercise. He wanted to lie down for several days after the torture he'd just endured, but he knew he would only walk again if he put in the effort.

But oh, how it pained him.

"I have not seen anyone come to visit you in the past weeks," Gweneth said slowly as she moved to straighten the pillows on the sofa, which were already straight enough. "I thought Nyana lived in the city."

"She does." He frowned as he massaged his legs from his ankles to his knees. "I already mentioned our relationship is strained."

"Because of your long absence from her life?" she ventured.

He nodded, trying to fight the guilt pinching him in the side. His absence hadn't been his fault. He knew that. But it was difficult to shoulder, nonetheless. "I don't know how to become a part of her life. And I suspect she doesn't know, either."

She moved from the sofa to the doorway and snatched two walking sticks, something between a cane and a crutch, and secured them to the back of his chair. "We'll need these real soon."

Her hand reached for her collar, but it slowly lowered, followed by a wave of sadness in her eyes. And only then did he sigh and run a hand down his face. "I entirely forgot."

He wheeled himself into the entry room, her following curiously behind. With a little difficulty, he reached for his coat from a tall hook and dug into each pocket until he found what he was looking for.

The playful side of him that had long since disappeared years ago resurfaced as he clasped her green brooch in his hand and hid it within the confines of his palm. A mischievous smile lifted on his lips as he held his hand up to her.

"Let's play a game, shall we? If you can guess what lies within my palm, I will give you anything you want."

"Anything?" She giggled, bending to peer closer at his hand. But not even an edge peeked out from his fingers. "And if I fail to guess correctly?"

"Then you get to make supper tonight."

"I make supper every night." A look of determination crossed her expression, and he couldn't deny that he loved her excitement in the face of a challenge, no matter how small. "How many guesses do I get?"

"Three."

"Sweets," she said immediately.

"Try again." Honestly, there was no possible way she'd guess correctly. But he wanted to see her smile again.

Gweneth tapped her fingers against her lips. "I have no idea what else could be small enough to fit in your hand." She shrugged her shoulders. "A button."

A grin grew across his face as he shook his head. "One more guess. I think I'm going to enjoy sitting back and watching you cook the entire meal."

She playfully swatted his shoulder. "If I guess correctly, *you* will make supper and *I* will sit back and watch."

"Fair enough." He gestured with his head toward his hand. "What will it be?"

"Give me a hint?"

"Are you trying to cheat?"

"No," she laughed. "But I wouldn't mind learning what a Forest Fae meal is like." She crossed her arms with one finger now tapping against her chin. "This one is a bit farfetched, but I'm going to go with a piece of jewelry."

Surprise lifted his brows at her guess. It was broad but correct. "Mother of autumn," he muttered with a mock pout. "It seems I am making supper tonight."

He opened his hand to reveal her brooch, but instead of an excited smile like he expected to find on her face, her chin trembled, and tears filled her eyes.

Slowly, her fingers caressed the smooth, green oval, brushing against his hand as she picked it up and cradled it against her heart. "How did you find this?" she rasped. "I never mentioned it was gone."

Ducking his head bashfully, he replied, "I noticed you wearing it during the interview, and I concluded it was something important to you. I bought it from a woman in the market. I didn't mean to keep it from you for so long. I simply forgot I had—"

He grunted in shock when she silenced his words with a kiss. His heart stuttered. His ears burned. His hands fell limp into his lap. He couldn't move. He couldn't react. Because never in his life had he expected to be kissed again. Especially not by a smart, beautiful, talented woman.

Gweneth broke the kiss all too suddenly. A flush climbed up her face and to her ears as he stared back at her, unable to form a coherent sentence let alone a single word on his tongue.

Her hand flew to her mouth. "I'm sorry!" she gasped. And then she spun around and fled from the room and up the stairs. A resounding bang shuddered the structure of the house before the entire atmosphere stilled.

For far too long, he stared after her while her kiss still tingled across his lips. And when his heart finally caught up with his mind, he dropped his head into his hands and focused on breathing deeply.

Fourteen years ago, Nyana and Meredith had been separated from him, and then Meredith had died. He'd lost so much in his life. To lose anything else he cared about would destroy him.

No, not anything. *Anyone.*

Warmth burned in his chest at the thought of Gweneth and the weeks they had spent together since her arrival. She was the sunlight in his life after a snowstorm that kept raging on and on. She'd brought laughter back into his life. Laughter and happiness and warmth.

But...

His legs demanded his attention, reminding him of his inadequacies and failures.

You are allowed to be happy again, his inner voice murmured inside his head. *Don't let Attleglade take any more from you.*

The fear of trusting, of loving again struck him straight through the chest until it stole his very breath. How could he love Gweneth when he knew she wanted a career? And not a relationship?

He pushed the terrifying thoughts from his mind and wheeled himself into the kitchen, banging pots and pans as he started preparing one of Attleglade's most common dishes—venison soup and tea bread. And while he cooked, his lips refused to stop tingling with Gweneth's kiss.

"I am out of practice," he scoffed to himself as he realized he'd simply froze up instead of returning her kiss. Perhaps if he got another chance, he wouldn't fail as spectacularly the second go around.

***

Supper was quiet.

After Gweneth had finally braved leaving her room, she'd joined Emeric at the dining table, neither of them speaking a single word from where they sat across from one another, eyes fixed on their food.

The tips of her ears burned with embarrassment, even hours after the incident earlier. She searched her mind for something to say. *Anything.* But it came up blank except for the humiliation she'd brought upon herself by kissing her patient.

She couldn't lie. She'd imagined kissing him several times. But in her fantasies, he'd never not responded, as if he'd wanted the kiss to end sooner rather than later. As if he were waiting politely for her to stop.

Forming any sort of attachments to her patients was always a line she refused to cross. Why, then, had she crossed it with Emeric? He hadn't even wanted it. She'd read the room wrong, and now she found herself wallowing in humiliation.

"Nothing to say?" Emeric asked, shattering the silence with the hammer of his voice.

Her head darted up, her mouth falling open as she stared wide-eyed at him. Embarrassment burned hotter through her body. "I-I-I-u-u-uh—"

"About the food," he said, nodding to her bowl. "You wanted to know what a Forest Fae dish tasted like. I'm sitting on the edge of my seat, terrified you hate it."

"A-a-ah." She cleared her throat, her hand darting to the brooch she had pinned at her neck once again, grasping it in her fingers. "It's more flavorful than I anticipated. What spices are inside?"

He disarmed her entirely as he smiled in her direction and waved his spoon at her. "It's an Attleglade secret. I'll never tell."

She wished she could laugh at his jest, but mortification continued to keep a firm hold on her tongue.

"I've been thinking about what you said," Emeric said slowly as he stirred his soup around in his bowl. "Perhaps I should stop waiting for Nyana to come around." He eyed her across the table. "Life has taught me to be cautious. To play it safe rather than take risks. Because when I take risks, I lose...so much."

Her lips parted for a shaky breath when she suddenly wondered if they were still talking about Nyana.

He continued to gaze intently at her. "I don't want to play it safe anymore, because I will never gain those things I could possibly lose in the first place." Finally, he averted his attention to his food. "Tomorrow, I'm planning on visiting Nyana at her home. I hoped you might accompany me. I usually have Bastien to diffuse the air but..."

Relief flooded through her at the calm waters Emeric created in which to sail her boat. Perhaps things didn't have to be awkward between them after all. "I would love to accompany you. I'm not sure I can outmatch Bastien's levity, but I can try."

"Levity." He snorted and waved his spoon at her again. "That boy is the biggest tease and the most infuriating troublemaker. If you meet him one day, you'll see. He shows his true colors immediately."

After witnessing Emeric's calm and collected demeanor, she couldn't easily imagine his offspring with a personality completely opposite. "How so?"

The man leaned closer across the table, his food forgotten. "Let me tell you about the time he brought home a squirrel and broke nearly everything in the house."

Over the next couple of hours, Emeric regaled her with stories of Bastien's exploits and calmed the anxiety in her soul with laughter. Despite the exasperation in his tone, his love for his son was clear in the way he spoke about him. The man was a natural-born storyteller, and she hung onto his every word.

In return, she traded stories about her time as a healer, both the amusing stories and a few incredulous tales. Her story-weaving abilities paled in comparison, but she delighted in being able to make him laugh a couple of times, and she enjoyed the sight of his smile far too much.

She easily pictured herself in the future with Emeric by her side as they traveled from kingdom to kingdom, him selling his wares and her offering healing services.

But then she sobered at the thought. She loved her career. For years, she had shunned relationships, pushing them aside to focus on herself and her career goals and her love for her patients. The path had never felt so lonely.

Until now.

But Emeric didn't want her, as evidenced by his non-reaction to her kiss.

He broke her out of her somber thoughts by reaching across the table and grabbing her empty dishes, balancing them on his lap with his own. "Do you play any instruments, Gwen?" he asked before wheeling himself toward the kitchen.

Hesitantly, she followed.

"Unfortunately, no. You mentioned you carve instruments. Do you play?"

Curiosity probed at her when he nodded and began rinsing the dishes beneath the water pump in the sink. "Almost every Forest Fae where I'm from plays some sort of instrument. I enjoyed playing the lute. I haven't strummed a chord in...a very long time."

The sudden slump in his shoulders spoke of his broken soul. True, Emeric was different from the man she had first met weeks ago. But he wasn't yet whole.

She clasped her brooch, her heart beating wildly as she asked with uncertainty in her tone, "Will you play for me?"

Emeric's entire body stiffened, and the sight of his unwillingness raked another cut across her heart. After today's earlier blunder, she never should have asked such a thing. Because she didn't like the feeling of putting herself on a layer of thin ice, only for it to break beneath her feet and dunk her in cold, miserable water.

"I have no idea if I can still play," he said instead of giving her a hasty rejection. "All of my belongings were burned in the fire meant to kill me." He paused and frowned. "My new carving is just that. A carving."

She ran a hand down her arm and cupped her elbow in her hand. "I understand if you don't want to show me."

He blinked at her as if slowly escaping the nightmares in his mind. "I do want to show you." As he wheeled himself back toward his room, she followed. "This is almost the only thing I've accomplished since leaving Attleglade. It takes a while to carve larger instruments."

Although she wanted to follow him inside his room, the incident earlier gave her pause. Instead, she found a place to sit on the sofa, waiting as drawers opened and closed in the other room, followed by a silent curse when his wheelchair must have bumped into furniture.

She held back a giggle.

Finally, he emerged with an instrument case and opened it to reveal a beautiful lute carved out of bone. Reverently, she reached out and ran her fingers across the eleven loose strings along the neck of the instrument, only for a chorus of off-tune notes to reverberate within the body.

He grimaced. "What a dreadful sound."

As if unable to help himself, he picked up the lute and tightened the strings one at a time, plucking each of them until a smooth, melodic note escaped. And then he strummed his hand down the length of the strings.

Gweneth's lips parted at the beautiful, soulful sound, a piece of her shocked Emeric could create such a heavenly chord within the matter of minutes.

"Play me something," she breathed.

He bit his lip, fingers hovering over the strings. But then his lips twitched as he met her eye. "You correctly guessed the surprise I hid in my hand earlier, and I promised you anything you wanted. Is this your wish? For me to play for you?"

The mortified heat burned her ears all over again as she recalled the incident with perfect clarity. She dipped her head and adjusted her spectacles to give something to occupy her hands with. Somehow, she managed to lift her head to look him in the eye. "Yes. But I wish for you to play only if you would like to."

"I do," he murmured. "Though, I'm not sure if I can remember how to do this."

He rested the body of the instrument beneath his arm while his fingers curled under the neck. He held on tenderly as if it were a child rather than a lute. "I don't know the words to this song in your language, only in my native tongue."

Her eyebrows rose with the realization that each word he spoke was tinged with the faintest accent. Until now, she hadn't realized he didn't usually speak in the Sun Fae tongue. But his nearly flawless execution told her he used to.

The man took a deep breath before he strummed his fingers across the lute, creating another melodic sound that cushioned her entire soul in a cocoon of warmth. He smiled, his previous anxiety visibly melting from his expression and leaving behind unadulterated joy.

As if his fingers remembered the movements, they plucked the strings one at a time. Slowly at first, and they moved quicker until each note blended into a beautiful melody.

And then he began to sing.

Gweneth swallowed the emotion that immediately slammed into her as his deep, alluring voice escaped his mouth like a rumble of a storm rolling through the sky. She didn't recognize the words he sang, so she listened to the melody and the rhythm. It captivated her with every rise and fall of his voice, with every expert strum of the lute.

Her attention moved from the lute to his face. A river of emotion moved across his expression, from joy to heartache to relief. And when he glanced up to meet her eye, her heart tumbled inside her chest at the sweetness in his silver eyes, at the adorable curve of his mouth as he sang, at the way he looked at her as if no one else existed.

Finally, his song finished with one final note reverberating through the room. It pulled on her soul like nothing ever had.

She didn't want it to end. Rather, she wanted him to play for her all night until she fell asleep with sweet rapture in her soul.

"You are full of surprises, Emeric Dalena," she whispered.

"Not too many more, I assure you," he jested, but then his expression turned serious after he set the lute back into its case.

He reached out to her, slowly, as if giving her time to pull away. But she didn't, because her breath caught, and her heart snagged when his fingers brushed against her cheeks as he slipped the spectacles from her face. Her surroundings blurred but his face remained focused.

"You have beautiful eyes." His gaze captivated her, tying her stomach in knots. "If you can heal me, how can you not heal you?"

"Not everything can be healed." She bit her lip self-consciously. Her spectacles had always created a pit of insecurity within her all her life. But never had they inspired fear like they did now. What did he think of them?

But he smiled as he gently slipped them back over her ears. "Then it's a really good thing they suit you."

Relief flooded through her. Of course, she didn't need his approval. But she wanted it.

Her entire body froze when he lowered his hands from her face and rested them on top of hers in her lap. The intent in his eyes burned every recess of her body, of her soul, until she feared she might light up in flames. Her heart beat with hope, nervousness, anticipation.

However, her hope deflated when he released her and bowed his head, a frown on his face. "Goodnight, Gwen. I am looking forward to our little excursion tomorrow."

Without another word, she watched as he disappeared into his bedroom and closed the door, leaving his lute behind.

The mortification previously running rampant through her now slowed into a somber disappointment. She'd never wanted to share her life with anyone. But the moment she found someone her soul longed for, that person didn't return her feelings.

Perhaps it was for the better to continue to focus on her career.

But the inward reassurance didn't erase the ache in her heart.

CHAPTER SEVEN

I AM STILL a coward.

Emeric's lips pressed tightly together as he wheeled his chair down the street with Gweneth at his side. The perfect opportunity to kiss her had arisen last night, to fix his previous blunder. But he'd frozen. Because he was afraid to take a chance.

He was already afraid to lose her. But he was terrified of experiencing another shattered heart when she would inevitably leave him in Ebriel and run toward her High Healer dreams.

He'd suffered enough broken hearts to last a lifetime. He didn't think he could manage another.

A frosty breath escaped on Gweneth's exhale as they turned the corner that led up a dirt path to Nyana's house. "I like this town. It's rather cozy."

"Not cozy enough," he countered. "It's too…open. Not enough trees."

Surprisingly, she laughed, filling the well of his soul with another bucket of life's simple joys. "What will make you happy, Em? Living inside your own tree in the middle of the city?"

Although he recognized the jest, he paused for a moment to give her a serious answer. "Yes," he replied with a nod as they made their way down the path with bare apple trees stretching endlessly on either side of them. "I would prefer living within a tree. I don't like having so much empty space."

When she didn't answer immediately, he glanced over at her to find her fighting a smile but losing in the end. She laughed again, this time squeezing his shoulder. Between his coat and her glove, heat still seemed to seep from her and into him.

"I can't possibly imagine what it's like. But I wouldn't mind learning."

A brief wind whispered through the boughs, calling his soul with a deep yearning for familiarity. "May I ask you something?" When she nodded, he still hesitated. He'd been wondering for many years now… "Is it even possible to reacquire my magic?"

She paused in her step before following beside him, this time at a slower pace than before. "How was it taken?"

"Through herbal sterilization." He grunted when his wheel momentarily lodged itself within a hole in the road, and with a strong heave of his arm, he managed to push himself out. "The council forced liquid down my throat."

A shudder ran through his body as he remembered the sudden helplessness, the insurmountable loss as if they'd severed several of his limbs rather than stripped him of his magic.

"I will need to take a closer look," she said slowly. "As in, uh, really close." He watched as a rosy blush spread across her cheeks, and the sight warmed him when he realized she was blushing for *him*. "Considering you lost it from a Forest Fae elixir, my guess would be that your magic has simply detached from your being and is floating aimlessly within your body. Now, if it had been taken with darker Shadow Fae magic, I don't think you'd ever see it again."

"So it's possible…"

"Yes. The answer is always yes."

Hope alighted in his chest, followed by amusement from her referencing his colder attitude toward her when they'd first met.

But then it was as if someone dumped a bucket of ice water over his head as he noticed the black carriage in front of Nyana's home, the side painted with the royal Sun Fae emblem—a twelve-pointed sun star.

Emeric swore and turned his chair around. He paused momentarily to grab Gweneth's hand and tugged her after him.

"What's wrong?" she asked, glancing over her shoulder. "Who is that?"

"Maisy's father. I don't think now is a great time—"

"Grandpapa!"

The front door of his daughter's house burst open, and moments later, auburn hair flew wildly behind his six-year-old granddaughter as she sprinted across the yard and jumped onto his lap, wrapping her arms tightly around his neck.

"I've been waiting and waiting and waiting until I got to see you again," Maisy said, her big blue eyes wide with excitement. "Mama said we could go to your house later today with Papa Calle, but you came to see us instead!"

"Papa Calle?" Gweneth breathed, her eyes wide now, too. "The king."

Before he managed a single word, Nyana gingerly descended the porch steps with all the grace of her mother before her. She looked far too much like Meredith, that each time he saw her, it momentarily stole his breath away.

"I am so happy to see you, Papa." Nyana embraced him and kissed his cheek before casting a curious glance in Gweneth's direction. "I apologize for not stopping by sooner. We've been preparing for Calle's visit."

Behind her, her husband, Joel, grabbed a wooden plank from the side of the house and rested it over the stairs as a ramp to give him access to the house. His eyes smarted at the kind gesture. Were all of the assumptions of their strained relationship in his head? He'd thought she didn't want to see him. But… He didn't feel like that was the case right now.

"Would it be better if I came back at another time?" he asked hesitantly, but before she answered, Calle stuck his head out of the house and smiled brightly, his shoulder-length auburn hair shifting with a tip of his head.

"Come on inside! Maisy and Eva just made ginger wafers. We're about to eat their hard work."

"Yay!" Maisy exclaimed, jumping off his lap just as Eva exited the house. Together, they ran inside hand in hand, and the others walked ahead, leaving him beside Gweneth.

"I'm so nervous," she whispered. "That's King Calle. I've only ever seen him from afar." She smoothed her clothing down. "Please explain this family to me. And fast. I don't understand who's related to who."

As they slowly followed after the others, Emeric whispered, "Nyana and Calle had a dalliance, which produced Maisy. He didn't know about her because his brother, Liam, faked his death and sent him to live in the Pits as a slave for six years. Liam forced Nyana into a marriage, which produced Eva." He took a deep breath and spoke quicker as they neared the house. "Calle escaped the Pits, and with the help of the valkyries, they ended Liam's wicked rule with his death. Calle married Skaja, one of the valkyries. Nyana married Joel, who is Calle's best friend, which produced baby Dylan."

His poor daughter. Fate hadn't been kind to her, but only now in Ebriel with Joel were things finally looking up.

With a good, rolling start, he managed to make it up the ramp and into the house on his own, and to his surprise, he found the valkyrie in question with her white-golden wings tucked behind her as she walked around the main room with baby Dylan in her arms. The woman's golden strands in her brown hair shimmered beneath the light coming in from the window, making her appear beautiful and harmless. But he'd seen the way she could move faster than a striking snake, an expert with a blade in her hand.

Calle approached immediately and shook his hand. "It's good to see you again, Emeric. The girls wanted to bring treats to you today, but it seems you beat us to it." He dropped his hand and shook Gweneth's next. "And who is your lovely companion?"

The room hushed, and Emeric felt everyone's stares as if they wanted to know the answer to his question, too.

He replied, "This is Gweneth Caddell. She's the High Healer who healed my legs."

Another hush, but this one was so silent that he could hear his own blood pulsing through his ears.

Calle's eyebrows furrowed as he glanced down at his legs, then his wheelchair, and doubt glazed over his expression. "Nyana told me the bones in your legs were shattered. Irreparable."

Emeric took in Gweneth's pinched mouth and the devastation hiding beneath her lidded eyes. Because this was her chance to achieve her dreams. And he was still in the chair. This didn't look good for her. And she knew it.

The last thing he wanted was to collapse in a room full of people, but picturing Gweneth's happy, radiant smile gave him the drive he needed. If this was what would make her happy, if becoming a High Healer at the Sun Palace was what she wanted more than anything, then he would do his best to give it to her.

He reached behind him to grab the two walking sticks attached to the chair.

As if realizing what he was about to attempt, Gweneth's eyes widened, and she lifted a cautioning hand. "Don't, Emeric. You don't yet have the strength you need."

"I have strength enough."

His legs shook as he willed his feet off the footrests and onto the floor, and a round of gasps filled the room just at the simple endeavor.

With both sticks braced against the ground, he shakily climbed to his feet. Gweneth rushed toward him, arms outstretched as if ready to catch him should he fall. But she didn't touch him.

He'd rather not have an audience for his first steps since the terrible incident, especially when he feared he would fall onto his backside like a baby learning to use their legs for the first time.

But the thought of Gweneth's happiness lended him the strength he needed. She'd given him the world by healing his legs. And now he would give it back to her by using them.

After so long of not being able to move his legs, they almost felt as if they were disjointed from his body. However, the exercises Gweneth had practiced with him every day for weeks helped make it possible to control them rather than for them to control him.

He willed his left leg forward, and in a long fourteen years, he took his first step.

Shouts of excitement lifted into the room, and his heart soared with happiness to witness his *family* giving him the encouragement he needed to take another step. They cheered wildly.

Laughter escaped him as he continued his slow trek to the opposite side of the room, and by the time he turned back around, his eyes filled to the brim with unshed tears. His legs shook with the effort of remaining standing, and he knew without a doubt he would fall if he didn't sit immediately.

Thankfully, Gweneth grabbed his chair and wheeled it toward him, and he sat heavily when his legs finally gave out.

He swiped a hand across his eyes. "I'm still unsteady," he said through everyone's excited chatter. "Gwen can't heal my weak muscles, but she fixed my bones."

Maisy jumped up into Calle's arms, and he held her on one hip as he addressed Gweneth. "Tell me. How many breaks were there?"

"Around two dozen on each side. The surgery took three days." She adjusted her spectacles. "With a few breaks in between, of course."

"Incredible," he breathed. "I have a little experience in healing, but nothing extensive. How were you able to harness the magic needed to do it over three days? It would have taken any normal healer weeks, perhaps even months, to accomplish what you did. And then again, regarding the extent of the injuries… This was an impossible surgery."

She smiled and glanced Emeric's way. "I like to believe nothing is impossible. And between everyone in this room, Your Highness, I have stored sunlight for years to recharge my magic quickly, so my patients don't have to wait."

"You can collect it yourself?"

Gweneth nodded.

Calle ran a hand over his jaw. "It's rare when I meet someone who has such power." He looked her over, almost as if regarding her in a new light. "One of our healers passed away a couple weeks ago, and we're looking for someone to take his place." But then he glanced between her and Emeric with uncertainty in the pinch of his mouth. "Do you have any interest in the position? I don't want to come between you and Emeric."

Heat flushed across Emeric's face, and he covered his eyes with his hand to try to hide it. Was it so obvious he had feelings for the Sun Fae? Was it so obvious that perhaps she had some for him, too?

He waited with bated breath for her answer. Because he wanted her to live her dream. But he feared losing her altogether.

When Gweneth didn't answer immediately, he glanced up to find her floundering, her mouth opening and closing as if unable to form an answer. And more than once, she looked his way.

He tried to smile through the pain. "All Gwen ever talks about is how much she wishes to become a High Healer at the palace. Of course, she'll take the position. She wants it more than anything."

A large smile spread across Calle's face as if Gweneth had answered herself. "Wonderful. I hope you might arrive within three weeks if it's not too much trouble. Let me know within two days if you change my mind, as that's when we're headed back to Heulwen."

The room erupted into excited laughter and chatter once more. He wheeled himself forward in an attempt to speak to Gweneth, but Nyana intercepted him. She grabbed the handles of his wheelchair from behind and steered him down the hallway and into another room, closing the door behind them.

Two beds lay on either side of the room, littered with lacy pillowcases and a dozen dolls each. A white canopy rested over one of the beds while a large and intricate model of a ship lay on the bedside table of the other.

He guessed the canopy bed belonged to Eva and the other belonged to Maisy.

"I'm so happy for you, Papa." Nyana embraced him tightly and regarded his legs with a sheen in her eyes. "What a miracle."

"Indeed, it is."

But then her expression shifted into curiosity as if trying to work out a puzzle in her mind. "Will you be accompanying Gweneth to Heulwen?"

He sighed as he stared into his lap and whispered, "I don't know."

"Does she know how you feel about her?"

"How do *you* even know how I feel about her? I've hardly said a single thing and we just arrived."

"Because," she squeezed his hand, "you used to look at Mama the way you look at Gweneth. There are a lot of things I've forgotten from my childhood, but I never forgot that."

Lifting a shaky hand, he covered his eyes again as he tried to push away the pain, as he tried to reject the emotions running rampant through his body. "Losing your mother destroyed me. I can't lose Gweneth. I'm terrified of hurting again."

Nyana knelt in front of him and slowly peeled his hand away from his face. Earnestness and love stared back at him in her blue eyes. "I know more than *anyone* how you feel, Papa. Before I met Joel, my life was more terrible than you could imagine. But I wouldn't change any of it. Because I am now married to the love of my life, and I have three beautiful children. My greatest trials have brought me my greatest happiness."

He voiced one of his most substantial fears. "What if she doesn't care for me?"

"Look her in the eye and ask yourself that again."

"That's what I'm afraid of."

"That she returns your feelings?"

He nodded. "I know it's silly. I'm terrified she won't have me, and I'm terrified she will."

And he felt even sillier for talking to his daughter about this, the very one whose relationship with him had been strained over the past year.

To try to better put his feelings into words, he amended with, "I want a life with her. I just don't know how to move forward."

She squeezed his hand. "With faith in yourself and hope for a brighter future. You just took your first steps in a very long time, Papa. Keep on walking forward, and you'll get there."

Releasing a long breath, he pulled his daughter into an embrace. "I am ever grateful for you."

"And I you."

They held each other for a few moments as Emeric fought off his emotions. One thread in the tangled web of his existence unraveled. And although he knew he had at least a dozen more to contend with, he was immensely happy that he was facing his challenges and overcoming them one by one.

"Let's not leave Gweneth with Calle for too long." He chuckled as he pulled away from her. "She might faint in his presence."

"I can't say she's the only one." She laughed alongside him. "It happened to me once as well."

His heart lifted as they shared a smile, and the lightened burdens on his shoulders was a strange and foreign sensation. His daughter was right. If he just kept walking forward, somehow, sometime, he would reach his destination.

CHAPTER EIGHT

"YOU ONLY HAVE one more day to back out," Emeric grunted from where he clung to the banister with white knuckles. "Are you sure you don't want to stay to aid a helpless man?"

Gweneth pinched his side. "If this is your way of trying to get me to live here permanently as your nurse, it's not working."

Oh, but yes. It was working wonders.

Her lips pressed tightly together as she ascended the next step with him at her side. He was getting stronger, as if the will to walk on his own was a bigger driving force than even yesterday. Getting offered the position of her dreams should have had her leaping with joy and crowing from the rooftops.

But the thought of accepting left a pit of discomforting ache in her stomach.

She didn't want to go anymore.

Because Emeric was here.

They ascended the last step together, and he turned to her, momentarily stopping her heart with the intensity of his silver eyes. A thrill shot through her at having to look *up* at him rather than *down*. He was taller than she expected, just the perfect height to wrap her arms around his waist and—

Emeric's legs suddenly collapsed from beneath him, and both of them cried out when he crashed to the ground at the top of the landing, bringing her down with him. She landed with a thud on soft carpet, staring up at the ceiling in a daze of surprise.

Beside her, Emeric said, "I think it's safe to say I'm good and stuck up here. No amount of coaxing will get me back down there."

Laughter burst out of her, and his promptly followed. But then the laugh slowly fizzled out when he turned onto his elbow and gazed down at her. Her stomach responded with a flutter, her heart with a dip as he touched her wrist with the softest brush. His fingers lightly traveled up her arm to her shoulder, and then he cradled her face with one hand.

Hard as she tried, she couldn't breathe.

He leaned down, but instead of shying away, his lips met hers in the sweetest caress.

She couldn't help herself from touching him, from running her hands up his arms, over his broad shoulders, and through his silky hair. The faintest moan escaped him, and she devoured it with her mouth as she returned his kiss.

Emotion trembled through her body from relief to joy to heartache. She couldn't go to Heulwen now. Not when her heart sang to the tune of his soul. Although she didn't know what kind of life she might lead at Emeric's side, she knew there was no other place she wanted to be.

Hot tears of happiness trailed down her face. As if he felt them run over his fingers, he wiped them away as he sprinkled several more kisses over her lips, giving her one last lingering kiss until they broke apart.

After the last incident, she never thought she'd be kissed by him again. But it had been better than she ever thought possible. Her heart responded with warmth and a seed of love. Because she cared for Emeric. Deeply. And his kiss had only planted the seed deeper and sprouted its leaves in a patch of warm sunlight.

"Did I do it right this time?" he asked in a husky tone.

"Perfectly right," she said with a contented sigh. "But feel free to practice any time you'd like."

He chuckled, and just the sight of his smile burst her heart into flames. She wanted to continue the kiss until the rest of her caught flames as well, but there was one thing she still needed to do...

"Lay down," she instructed softly, not wanting to break the fragile atmosphere with anything louder.

With a confused expression, he did as she asked and laid back on the plush carpet stretching from one end of the hallway to the other. She knelt over him and tried to ignore the way heat sparked against her fingers as she unbuttoned his shirt halfway and pushed the fabric aside.

"What are you doing?"

"Hush now," she chided, her mouth lifting in the faintest grin as she placed both her hands over the smooth but chiseled skin of his chest. Tendrils of her magic entered his body, searching, seeking. And when she didn't find what she was looking for, she delved deeper.

Her brows furrowed in concentration, and she closed her eyes as she continued her search. Only a few times had she worked with those who had lost their magic. In two of those cases, the magic had been gone entirely. In the third case, the woman's magic had run from her efforts to catch it but catch it she had.

"What happens when you try to call on your magic?" she asked, eyes still closed.

She felt his heart race beneath her touch as he answered, "It doesn't respond. It's as if nothing is there."

"Do you know if your people have ever dipped their toes into Shadow Fae magic?"

She opened her eyes the slightest bit to find him shaking his head. "Never. They are too proud to accept anyone else's culture."

Her lips pressed together when she still couldn't locate any sign of magic within his body. "You were the chief. Do you know what they put in the elixir?"

Another nod before he listed off the ingredients. One of them was a poison to kill magic, to dwindle it to nothing until it disappeared entirely. Although it wasn't shadow magic, it was still an effective poison.

"The bad news is your magic isn't simply detached from your body like I previously expected." Her magic continued to rummage through him like a hound dog following an old scent. "The good news is that in many cases, this poison never kills the magic completely, but gives the appearance that it does. Stay here."

She pushed on his chest to help her stand before rushing down the stairs. Without grabbing a coat, but only slipping her feet into her boots, she stepped outside into the chilly winter air, eyes searching the vicinity for some sort of plant that flourished during harsh weather.

Rounding the house, she finally spotted a handful of white and pink snowbalms climbing a trellis. She plucked two stems of the bell-like flowers, watching as they hung from white vines like bells hanging in a church.

Upon entering the house once again, she barely managed to kick off her boots before pulling on her healing gloves and jogging up the stairs, taking them two at a time. Emeric still lay where she'd left him, and without preamble, she placed a snowbalm stem in either of his hands.

"To possibly draw it out," she explained.

"Do I need to do anything?"

She didn't miss the hopeful lilt of his voice hidden beneath a layer of fear. "If you feel your magic, grab it. If you don't, then it's my job to find it for you."

If it's there, she added silently.

With the steady concentration her gloves offered her, she drew upon her magic. The sun stones glowed faintly beneath her administration as she wheedled her power into him once again.

Taking a deep breath, she closed her eyes and moved her magic along his spine and chest where the center of magic was located within each person. Only too late did she want to smack herself in the head when she realized she should have done this another time rather than right after their incredible kiss. If she declared him magicless, then the disappointment was sure to crush him.

Emeric inhaled sharply. "Right there. Try again right there."

She moved her efforts backward and continued her search, only to find the faintest trace of magic. Only a pinprick. But it was there.

"I need to feed your magic," she stated in her no-nonsense healer tone. "It shouldn't hurt, but it will make you feel…uncomfortable? Like you ate too much during a feast." She steadily focused her attention on the pinprick. Giving it light. Giving it life. "If you need me to stop at any time, let me know."

The small bit of magic latched hungrily onto her power, and she grunted as she braced herself against its devouring flame. It tried to steal what she possessed, fighting with all its might to survive. But she only allowed it morsels of her healing, a little bit at a time.

His magic grew steadily as she coaxed it out of the shadows. Emeric gasped, arching his back, his fists clenched.

"Should I stop?" she asked.

He only managed a shake of his head, and she continued feeding it with a steady hand.

Sun Fae like herself recharged their magic with sunlight. Shadow Fae recharged theirs in the moonlight. But Forest Fae, at least those descended from nymphs like Emeric's people, recharged their magic with the essence of the earth mixed with positive emotion.

A part of her wondered if a lack of happiness had made his situation worse.

All at once, it felt as if her magic exploded within him until it depleted entirely. A rush of energy exited her body. She gasped, the sound followed by a thick, overbearing silence.

Her jaw slackened, and she sat back on her heels, stunned as she watched his chest rise and fall with each breath. "I-I-

I'm sorry," she stammered, eyes wide. "I don't know what happened."

Had she fed his magic too fast? Too full? Had she destroyed any chance he had at gaining back his ability?

Slowly, Emeric slid his arm across his face until it covered his eyes, but she still caught the sheen of moisture trailing down his cheeks.

She squeezed her eyes shut, a shuddering breath escaping her as she bowed her head with regret. A healer was meant to help, not harm. And she feared she may have hurt Emeric, the one person she wanted to help more than anything.

Emeric's gentle fingers brushed against her cheek, and she felt him tuck something between her ear and spectacles. She barely dared to open her eyes, only to inhale sharply when his touch caused the snowbalms to grow eagerly, flowering over her head until they formed a crown of white, petal bells.

"What?" she gasped. "I thought…"

But her words trailed off when he wrapped his arms around her shoulders and pulled her against the warmth of his chest. Relief settled over her, followed by a raging fluster as he ran a hand down her back and held tightly onto her waist.

It wasn't the caress of an acquaintance but something so much more.

"You are…extraordinary," he murmured into her hair.

Her entire body warmed with his declaration, with the quiet rumble of his chest when he spoke, and she couldn't help herself from clutching tight onto the front of his shirt.

"I'm only doing my job," she said quietly, but the way she clung to him as if he were her sunlight bellied her words.

"You will make an even bigger name for yourself in Heulwen. People will flock to you just to experience your healing touch."

The thought of leaving him created a pit of panic in her belly. She wanted him. She needed him. In her life. Everyday. No matter what she had to give up to accomplish that.

Her expression crumpled as her hands traveled up the sturdy muscles of his chest, and she threaded her fingers through his hair. "Tell me now if you want me to stop. I don't want you to reject me again."

"I never meant to the first time," he replied in an equally husky tone. "I never thought I would be kissed again in my lifetime. You took me by surprise."

"Then I count myself fortunate, indeed." She kissed one side of his mouth and then the other. "That other women didn't discover the handsome man in the chair before I did."

Laughter erupted from him, and she promptly devoured the sound of it with her lips. His touch, his kiss filled her with immense warmth. She drank him in as if he were sunlight and her magic was starving.

A heady breath escaped her when he pulled her onto his lap and held her securely around the waist. She ran her hands up his chest, feeling each dip and groove of his muscles, and slipped them beneath the fabric of his shirt to his sturdy shoulders.

One by one, Emeric pulled the pins out of her hair until the brown waves cascaded down her shoulders, and with equally careful hands, he set her glasses aside as well. She inhaled sharply when he dug his fingers into the long locks and gently pulled her head back to expose the delicate skin of her neck. A trail of fire followed in his wake as he kissed along her throat, to her jaw, and then nipped on her ear.

"Emeric!" she gasped, followed by a giggle.

But when he pulled her even closer, he effectively silenced her words with another passionate kiss. As she roamed her hands over his back, shoulders, and through his hair, it wasn't enough. She wanted more. To be even closer to him. To taste him. To breathe his air.

She wasn't sure who acted first as they deepened the kiss, tongue's exploring and breaths gasping. He tasted like sweet, fresh pine, filling her with more longing to taste every inch of him.

He flipped her over in a smooth movement until she lay on the carpet on her back.

"I'm sorry," Emeric panted a breath above her lips. "I should slow down."

"I don't want you to." She pulled him back down and they resumed their fiery kiss. She stripped him of his shirt and tossed it aside, and he unbuttoned her dress, kissing each new inch of exposed skin from her collarbone to her navel until the fire in her belly was nearly too much to handle.

All her life, she'd never put focus and energy into romantic relationships. But with Emeric, it felt right. She would fight for this, for a life with him, because she wanted it more than anything.

CHAPTER NINE

A PEACEFUL FIRE billowed in the hearth, casting its warmth across Emeric's bare skin as he held Gweneth in his arms. They lay together on a soft, woven rug, a blanket covering them.

Their heads rested against the same pillow, her hair fanning over the cushion and pressing against his nose.

He breathed in deeply, inhaling her sweet scent. His fingers lightly caressed her bare arm from her elbow to her wrist, tracing her palm, and intertwining with her fingers. Her hands were soft like the rest of her.

"I'm so tired but I don't want to sleep yet," she murmured sleepily before she pulled his hand closer to her face and kissed his knuckles.

"I know the feeling." He kissed her shoulder and sighed with a deep happiness echoing in the chambers of his soul. "I want to lie with you here all night."

"At least what remains of it." She chuckled, and he smiled at the beautiful sound. "In the morning, I'll cook you a magnificent breakfast."

He brushed her hair aside and kissed her ear. "Thank autumns," he said, lips pressed against her skin. "I don't think my legs will be moving anytime soon. I'm feeling unbelievably sore."

Another laugh escaped her, and this time, she turned over until she faced him with those beautiful hazel eyes gazing straight through his heart and into his soul. "Don't tell a healer such things; otherwise, you are going to receive a bit of relief."

"Don't expend your magic." Or what was left of it for the day after she'd healed his magic. "You're already tired."

But she ignored him, and a cooling relief chased away the aching burn in his legs until drowsiness finally washed over him without the ache and stiff muscles to keep him from falling asleep.

He sighed and murmured his thanks as his arm moved to wrap around her waist. "You are one of the most beautiful women I've ever met."

Inside and out. Her outer beauty. Her inner kindness, dedication, and perseverance. She was unlike anyone he'd ever met, and he cherished her for it. He counted himself the luckiest man that fate chose to send her to him. Because now he never wanted to let her go.

Sleep quickly claimed him, only for him to wake up seemingly minutes later with the sunlight cascading through the windows, chasing away the previous darkness. The hearth's flame had long since dwindled to nothing, leaving behind the faintest chill of morning.

He sat up groggily, his gaze searching the vicinity for any sign of Gweneth. But the room was empty, and he heard no signs of her stirring within the house.

The scent of apple muffins and cooked eggs brought his attention to the tray lying on the low table near his line of sight. A piece of folded parchment lay on top. He reached for it and carefully unfolded it, his brows furrowing when he stared back at the Sun Fae's written language. It took a few moments for him to adjust to reading in something other than his native tongue.

Headed to the makret, be back soon.
Gwen ♡

He smiled at the endearing way she mixed up her letters again. It was what got them in this mess in the first place, but that little mix-up about her age was one of the biggest blessings in his entire life.

Gweneth Caddell had healed his body, his spirit, his heart. She'd left an imprint on his soul in a way no other person had before. Although it was impossible to pay her back for what she'd done for him, he knew helping her get her dream job at the Sun Palace at least made up for the smallest fraction.

He owed her the moon. And throughout his life, he hoped to give it to her.

Reaching for his walking sticks, he grunted as he used them to push himself to his feet. Only a couple days ago, he might have collapsed immediately, but the muscle-building exercises were enough to keep him standing. For now. Who knew how long his strength would last?

He slowly ambled to his room and dressed himself in a new pair of clothes, all while memories of his time with Gweneth last night burned into his heart and filled him with happiness.

A smile lifted on his lips as he dug into his bedside table and pulled out his latest carving. The ring was crafted of cattle bone, weaved in an intricate way to look like white lace but sturdy enough to withstand everyday wear.

A part of him feared she would reject him when the time came, but after last night, he was almost certain she wouldn't.

Wanting to hold onto the hope for his future, he slipped the ring into his pocket and returned to the front room where the breakfast sat on the table. He started to reach for the muffin when his hand froze, and ice jolted through his blood.

The pantry was full, as Gweneth had gone to the market two days ago. And unless she was spending the wage he gave her despite her insistence that she didn't want it...

He shot upright fast enough for him to wince as the sudden movement tugged on the muscles in his legs. Today was the day Calle was to leave for Heulwen, the last day for Gweneth to change her mind about accepting the job as a High Healer.

Gweneth wasn't going to the market.

She was going to turn down her dream job.

For him.

"No!" he hissed as he stumbled toward the door and threw it open. He didn't stop to grab a coat or shoes, but rather rushed outside with only a pair of socks to protect him from the frozen ground. His legs trembled with the effort of keeping himself upright, even with a walking stick in each hand. But panic drove him forward, a desperation to keep her from making the biggest mistake of her life.

After a rickety journey down the stone steps and a wobbly trek on the frozen dirt road, he realized he couldn't get to his daughter's house without either falling flat on his face partway there or not making it in time before the deed was done.

His gaze traveled up the tree near his home, to the tall boughs bereft of leaves.

At one time in his life, he'd flown from tree to tree with the strength of his legs and the use of his magic. But the trees in Attleglade were larger with thicker branches, and his magic hadn't felt quite so new.

Determination slammed into him as he threw his walking sticks to the ground, and they clattered against the road.

Whereas his muscles needed time to gain strength, his magic was like an innate part of him to create and mold as he desired. When he asked, it eagerly obeyed.

He reached inside his well of magic to find it full rather than dwindling into the quiet unknown. And with the faith of his youth, he commanded it.

A tree branch shot toward him in a limber movement and wrapped around his waist. His head nearly snapped back with whiplash as the branch pulled him into its boughs as if hugging him like a long-lost friend.

When it stilled, his feet struggled to find purchase against slippery bark, and he grasped wildly for branches around him to steady himself.

He blew out a long, frosty breath. It had been a very long time since he'd connected with his element. He needed to let go and let his instinctual magic do the work. Because if he allowed fear to take over, he would not succeed.

He forced himself to glance down at the ground far below and assess the distance of the potential fall. He assessed. And then he accepted. If he made a mistake, he could fall and injure or kill himself. But he was a Forest Fae. Sprinting through the treetops and even falling safely was pounded into them nearly since birth.

Clenching his teeth, his brows furrowed as he commanded the tree to lift him higher. And after only a moment's pause, he ordered it to throw him.

Cool wind whipped against his face, grabbing his hair and clothing as he soared through the air. Branches parted for him to avoid scratching him before the next tree caught him smoothly around the waist.

If only his legs were strong, this wouldn't be as difficult.

Not giving himself time to back out, he launched himself again and again until he soared fluidly through the air as if he were born with wings. One after the other, trees caught him and launched him across Ebriel.

When one of the trees proved to be too far, he cried out in alarm and squeezed his eyes shut, bracing himself for a rough impact. But it never came when a tree branch snatched him from the air and cradled him within its boughs as if he were a baby.

A trembling breath left his lips as he commanded the tree to lift him higher, and it tossed him into Joel's and Nyana's apple orchard.

The trees were much closer together this time, allowing him to use his arms instead of relying purely on the willingness and strength of the boughs. He swung from tree to tree with help here and there. And when he spotted a familiar figure walking down the road, his breath hitched as he moved faster, with more purpose.

Branches groaned as he neared, which must have alerted Gweneth to his presence. She glanced up right as he dropped down from the tree nearest her, a branch wrapped around his waist to help keep him steady.

The shock in her eyes slowly melted into guilt hunched into her shoulders. She was on her way *toward* the house and not *away* from it. He wasn't too late.

"Don't. You. Dare!" he thundered with heaving breaths. "I will not allow you to throw away this opportunity."

She held her hands to her heart, devastation hiding behind the spectacles over her eyes. "I love you, Emeric Dalena," she said in a raspy, fervent tone. "More than my career. I will gladly give this up to stay with you."

Shock coursed through him as he stared back at her. They had known each other for weeks now, lived under the same roof, shared laughter, meals, and kisses. She was in every essence one of the most incredible women he'd ever met, and his heart sang a duet with her soul. But hearing the words from her mouth took him aback. Because for so long, he'd resigned himself to a lonely existence. To live as the shell of a man he used to be, only to disappear into the cold finality of death alone.

But love?

He'd felt so worthless for so long, and he never thought he'd hear the words from someone other than his family again.

Especially not from a beautiful, talented woman like Gweneth.

Slowly, the flames of happiness, of determination melted the icy shock from his frigid veins as he managed a step forward, and then another with the tree still helping to support his weight.

"And you don't think I would go with you?" He brushed the back of his fingers against her cheek.

"What about your family? Nyana is here. Your grandchildren."

Perhaps he was selfish, but… "I have lived my entire life for them. It's time I live my life for me." His fingers moved to brush along her neck. "And what I want is to travel with you and go on adventures with you and support you as you reach your career dreams. I know I may not be strong yet, but I will be soon. I swear I won't slow you down—"

"I don't care one wick about how slow you travel at my side…" She gripped his hand and squeezed. "…as long as we do it together."

He swallowed against the nervousness running rampant through his belly as he dug into his pocket and pulled out the ring he'd carved from his pocket. The intricate lacy bone matched the strength and delicateness of the woman before him.

"Em…" she breathed.

A chilly wind rushed through the orchard and sent shivers down his spine with his little protection against the elements. But it didn't deter him from speaking his heart.

"I intended to ask for your hand far later than now, but…perhaps you might consider a life at my side. A new start for both of us. Whatever that looks like." Afraid she might reject him, he spoke faster now, not giving her a chance to say anything. "I never thought I would find love again. I never thought I would find happiness. But with you, I feel whole. Complete. You make me want to be better, to see the possibilities of life around me." He swallowed when emotion threatened to overcome him, especially as her lovely eyes filled with tears. "I love you so much. And I hope you will stay by my side. As my wife."

Gweneth lifted her spectacles to wipe her eyes before she gave him a watery smile. "I knew I wanted to stay the first moment I forced the front door open with my foot."

He laughed. "I've never met a pushier woman."

"Not pushy," she corrected with a wink. "Just determined to get what I want."

"And…what do you want?"

Her smile widened as she held out her left hand to him. "To find out if that ring fits."

Releasing an anxious breath, he slipped the ring onto her finger and sighed in relief when it fit. In Attleglade, he'd carved plenty of jewelry, and at one point acquired the skill to guess the correct finger size. But the one time it mattered the most, he was glad he got it right.

He opened his mouth to speak but she wrapped her arms around his neck and pulled him into a kiss.

Between kisses, she said, "You're not even wearing shoes! Let's get you out of the cold and to Nyana's house."

He broke the kiss and stared at her with confusion. "But I thought you weren't going to turn the job down."

She laughed and ran a hand down his arm. "No, no, no. First, we need to announce our engagement to the people you love. And perhaps we might convince Calle to give us a ride back to your home. I'm not flying through the boughs with you."

"Then you're missing out." He pulled her close and kissed her again. "I know my family will accept you with open arms."

CHAPTER TEN

THE NEXT TWO weeks were filled with wedding planning and packing and lots of exercises to strengthen his body to prepare for the journey to Heulwen. Emeric now walked on his own without the aid of a wheelchair or walking sticks. Although he still tired easily, he no longer collapsed or ambled about on unsteady legs.

Emeric forced the last crate of dinnerware closed to take only what they needed to their home in the sun city. Calle had generously gifted them a large plot of land on which to live, and Emeric could hardly wait to dig his fingers into the soil and bring a home to life with his very own magic. He only needed a single seed, but he thought he could find *something* to purchase in the city when the time came.

Gweneth was more excited than he expected a non-Forest Fae would be to live within the confines of a tree. But he swore to carve it out to her liking and make it a beautiful, cozy home.

For the two of them. Together.

His chest warmed at the thought.

"Em!" Gweneth's voice shouted from the stairs, followed by footsteps descending to the main floor. "Have you seen my portmanteau? I seem to have misplaced it in the excitement of packing."

She entered the kitchen, and he took that moment to grab her around her waist and pull her flush against him.

"I think it can wait," he murmured against her ear, softly trailing kisses down her neck.

She giggled when he ran his tongue over the ticklish spot between her shoulder and throat. But rather than pushing him away, she pulled him closer and released a contented sigh.

Slowly, he backed her up until he pinned her against the wall. It felt good to have so much control over his body. Instead of hanging useless, his legs were filled with strength he had not experienced in many years.

"I suppose the packing *can* wait."

They met in another kiss, this one filled with the heat of passion. He didn't think he would ever tire of the way her touch left a trail of flames in their wake or the way her kiss filled him with intense longing.

He cupped the back of her knee and lifted her leg to his waist, trailing kisses along her jaw to her throat and across her collarbone. Her fingers quickly worked to unbutton his shirt, and his desire intensified as she ran her hands over his chest and teasingly hooked her thumbs in the waistband of his trousers.

Oh, how he loved this woman—

"Autumn winds!" a familiar voice gasped in his native tongue behind him.

Emeric dropped Gweneth's leg and spun around fast enough to give himself a headache, only to find his son staring at them with his mouth open, his wife, Seraphina, equally rooted in place with shock a step behind him.

"Bas!" Emeric cried as he hastily buttoned his shirt, all while his face burned with the heat of fluster. He continued speaking in the Sun Fae language so Gweneth could understand them. "Don't you at least have the decency to look away?"

"Uhhh...no?" Bastien glanced back and forth between them, followed by a lingering stare on his legs before he, too, switched tongues as he ran a confused hand through his long, white hair. "I don't understand! You're standing? Walking? Kissing a strange woman?"

Out of all the times for his son to show up unannounced, this was the worst. It was so like him. "The least you could have done was knock."

"I did!"

"No, you didn't," Seraphina said with a growing smirk, her white and brown wings lightly fluttering from where they draped against her back, a stark contrast to the black of her hair and lips. "You walked right in."

"All right, so I didn't. But how was I supposed to know you'd be catching embers with a woman in your kitchen?"

With a sigh of lingering embarrassment, he gently took hold of Gweneth's hand and guided her closer to the other two. "This is Gweneth Caddell. She's a High Healer Sun Fae. And she's…uhh…my fiancée."

A smile slowly grew across Bastien's face as he glanced between the two of them. "I see what's going on here. You fell in love with the woman who healed your legs!"

Emeric's face flamed with heat, and he tried to hide his embarrassment with his hand. He'd wanted to approach this situation delicately with Bastien, not find himself thrown under the cart and run over several times as he tried to catch his breath.

But Bastien took it in stride as he grasped one of Gweneth's hands. "It's good to meet you, Gwen. I'm Bastien. I hope you've heard lots of good things about me."

"Well…" She smiled despite the obvious fluster in her pinched mouth as she tucked a strand of hair behind her long ears. "I've heard plenty about you. Lots of the mischief you've gotten yourself into as well."

"Someone needed to keep Pops on his toes. His life would have been *bor-ring* without me." He turned back to him, hands on his hips. "When's the wedding? We're only visiting for a week, so it better be sooner rather than later."

"I…uhh…" His fluster twisted his tongue until he could barely push words out of his mouth.

Thankfully, Gweneth stepped in for him. "We had planned a wedding in Heulwen in two months to make sure you and Seraphina were able to attend. But…" She shrugged and adjusted her spectacles. "Why not marry in Ebriel? The family is here."

"Everyone except Calle," Emeric reminded when his tongue finally untwisted. "It would not be fair to leave him out."

Bastien clapped his hands and rubbed them together. "Road trip to Heulwen, the lot of us. I haven't ridden in a carriage in…" He rubbed his chin as if deep in thought. "Probably close to sixteen years."

"Then how did you get here?"

"I ran." He grinned and gestured to Seraphina with his chin. "And she flew."

"And I won," Seraphina added with an elbow to Bastien's ribs, the perfect smirk to match his own.

Emeric shook his head. "It was a race?"

"Of course." His son waved away his surprise before turning to his wife. "But you only won because of the snow."

"I did not." Seraphina sidled closer to Bastien and tapped his chest with a finger. "Winged fae are naturally faster than those on the ground."

"Not if those winged fae are up against Forest Fae. Just wait until springtime. I will win against you fair and square."

Heated stares passed between the other two, both competitive and passionate, and Emeric wasn't sure if they were about to trade blows or *trade blows*. There was never any telling with them.

He gripped Gweneth around the arm. "Let's go before one of them implodes. Always bickering, the two of them."

"Come now, Pops." Bastien's grin widened as he stole him away from Gweneth and led him into the entry room. "Let's see how well those legs work."

"Go easy on me," he warned. "It will be a while yet until I'm at full strength."

But instead of testing the resilience of his legs, his son turned on him and lowered his voice, his silver-blue eyes sparking with curiosity. "When did all of this happen? How did you meet her? What did she do to heal your legs? I want to know everything."

For years, Bastien had been his support, and he suspected letting go of that role wasn't easy.

He glanced toward the kitchen to find Gweneth and Seraphina in a hushed conversation of their own. "She broke every warped bone in my legs and healed them properly. And…" The heat of pride flared in his chest as he commanded the snowbalms outside his home, and small vines slithered through the cracks in the window, blossoming their white blooms before their eyes.

"You got your magic back," Bastien gasped.

He nodded. "I accepted the application of a live-in nurse and ended up with a fiancée." He paused to bite his lip. "She's wonderful. If you just get to know her—"

"I already love her because you do." Bastien embraced him, causing a flood of emotion to wash through him. "I'm so happy for you, Pa." He held him at arm's length. "Truly."

"Your blessing means everything to me." He cleared his throat. "I know she's not your mother, but..."

Bastien squeezed his shoulder. "There's always room for another mother. Seraphina has three fathers after all." His son chuckled and stretched his arms over his head. "You deserve to be happy." His eyes snapped open. "Oh!"

Digging into the satchel at his waist, Bastien pulled out a small glass vial and placed it into Emeric's hand.

Emotion clogged his throat, and he swallowed several times as he attempted to keep it at bay. Within the small vial lay a single seed the size of his fingernail. He'd recognize it anywhere, as it was the very foundation of the tree he'd carved out for himself and Bastien to live in many years ago.

"I know you swore to never set foot in Attleglade again," Bastien said, scratching his chin. "So, I went for you. A few pinecones survived the fire at our old place, and I extracted one of the living seeds." He chuckled and ran a hand over the back of his neck. "It looks like you might not have to hire someone else to grow it for you after all."

"Bas..." Emeric croaked before pulling him into another embrace. "Thank you for this thoughtful gift."

Bastien waved away his thanks, running a hand over his neck again like he did when he was flustered and didn't know what to say. He backed out of the room and climbed the stairs with Seraphina, likely finding a vacant room to sleep in later that night.

Moments later, Gweneth joined his side and elbowed him in the ribs. "You never mentioned Bastien is charming."

"Oh, his charm fades away fast, I assure you. Give him ten minutes, tops, before he'll do something to question your entire judgment about his character."

Gweneth laughed and squeezed his arm. "I highly doubt it's as bad as you say. Seraphina seems completely enamored with him."

"Ten minutes," he emphasized, smiling at the thought of his son despite everything. "And a fair warning, he will talk your ear off if you let him. That boy loves the sound of his own voice."

Another laugh as they headed back toward the kitchen. Not to resume their earlier activity, unfortunately, but he imagined their new guests might enjoy a cup of warm tea.

Just as he placed a teapot on the stove to boil, Bastien called for the two of them. Except...his voice sounded as if it came from outside.

They each pulled on a pair of shoes and shrugged their coats on before exiting the house. A light snowfall cascaded from the white skies, each snowflake dancing with graceful leaps and twirls. He'd always loved the quiet stillness winter brought each year. Despite the cold, he often found a cozy place to enjoy the scenery while sipping on a hot cup of tea.

"You can see the entire city from up here!" Bastien shouted from above him, bringing his attention to his lithe form standing confidently on the edge of the roof. He pointed in the distance. "I think I even spot Nyana's place."

Gweneth inhaled sharply and clutched onto his wrist. "He's on the roof!"

"Don't worry," Emeric reassured. "The trees in Attleglade are much higher."

But his words did nothing to erase the distress in her eyes. Surely, she'd seen plenty of fall injuries in her healing career. Possibly even a few fall deaths as well.

"Whoa!" Bastien cried out as he slipped on a patch of ice on one of the shingles. Gweneth's scream drowned in his ears as Bastien fell the distance from the roof to the ground. Only to roll into the fall and smoothly onto his feet. An enormous grin stretched across his face as he pointed to her. "Gotcha! You fell hard for that one."

Gweneth's hand rested over her heart, and she appeared both murderous and sick.

Emeric rolled his eyes. Yes, he still worried over his son, but he'd seen Bastien fall from greater heights and make it out without a single scratch. Besides, that fall had looked intentional. "Remember what I said about showing his true colors immediately?" He gestured to Bastien. "Imagine living with this terror all your life."

"You were right," she gasped, clutching tighter to him as if she might topple over. "It took less than ten minutes for him to scare my heart out of my chest."

"Oh, come now, Gwen." Bastien wrapped his arm around her shoulders and squeezed. "If we're to be family, you have to learn to have a bit of fun."

She and Emeric shared an exasperated look, almost as if she only just realized what she got herself into by agreeing to marry him.

"I always say you're going to be the death of me, Bastien." He shook his finger at his son. "I still mean it."

Bastien waved away his words with a flippant hand. "Twenty-two years and still going strong."

Emeric laughed and shook his head, and he reckoned he must not have laughed often because the sound seemed to startle Bastien. He dropped his arm from Gweneth's shoulders, giving him a shocked stare. At least until a grin pulled up on his lips and he laughed in tandem.

"Well, I'm off to bed. Ser and I raced through the night, and we're tired."

With one final wave, Bastien returned to the house. It never ceased to amaze him how much endurance his son had built up over the years as a patrol guard for Attleglade. Surely, he was giving his new wife a run for her money.

"Change of plans, I suppose?" Gweneth turned her face into his chest and wrapped her arms around his waist.

It felt good to hold her properly. Rather than a wheelchair or walking sticks between them, he held her within the protection of his arms, where their bodies fit perfectly together as if they were meant to find each other all along.

He kissed the top of her head and smiled into her hair. "With Bastien in your life, you have to learn to be flexible. Let's find out if Nyana and the family can make it to Heulwen on short notice."

"For you, I'm sure they can make the journey."

"For *us*," he rectified, brushing a strand of hair out of her face that the wind had worked out of her updo. "You're family now, too."

She tipped her head up and kissed him. "I like the sound of that."

CHAPTER ELEVEN

"JUST A FEW more steps," Emeric murmured in her ear.

A blindfold lay across Gweneth's eyes, and she walked blindly forward as he led her from behind. Nerves rolled in her stomach, not just because this was the start of her new life with her new husband, but because she knew how important it was to Emeric for her to love their home.

But quite honestly, she had no idea what to expect.

A chilly exhale escaped her when they stopped, and the gentle tugging at the back of her head indicated Emeric was untying the knot in the blindfold. A moment later, it dropped from her eyes.

And her lips parted as her breath caught.

She stood in front of an enormous tree with boughs stretching endlessly toward the sky. It was at least a hundred times larger than any tree she'd seen in her lifetime. Impossibly large. Impossibly beautiful.

Small strands of blue crystals decorated the branches, emitting a soft glow in the semi-darkness of evening, revealing the closed window shutters at different levels in the tree. Even more amazing, the tree was alive. The amount of skill to create a house inside a living tree was incredible.

"I'm speechless," she breathed.

For a moment, he studied her as he bit his lip. "A good speechless or bad?"

"Definitely good."

He released an audible breath and took her hand. "I'll show you the inside."

In a sudden swoop, he picked her up into his arms, and she held tightly onto his neck. Carrying his own weight was one thing. Carrying someone else was another matter entirely. But Emeric seemed determined to cross the threshold of their new home with Gweneth in his arms no matter if he stumbled a couple of times.

She giggled as he glanced from the door handle, to her, and back to the door handle. Just as she started to offer to open it herself, a vine whipped out from the boughs, pulled on the handle, and pushed the sturdy wooden door open for them.

"There!" Emeric declared triumphantly. "I told you I can do this."

And then in another step, he carried her over the threshold of the magnificent tree he had grown and hollowed out within the space of a week. Bastien and Nyana had helped him while keeping it a secret of what lay within.

Never in her life had she seen a Forest Fae dwelling.

And the sight of her own awed her.

Frost blooms stretched across the walls and ceiling of the main floor, which was carved out in a circular fashion. The furniture was a part of the tree, carved from the walls or ceiling. Crystal sconces rested on the walls, a soft blue light emanating from the beautiful gems. A couple of shutters lay closed, but when the season warmed, she was sure they would allow beautiful natural light to enter the home. And the *scent!* Earthy. Woodsy. And judging by the grin growing across his face, it must have been nostalgic for him.

He set her down, just barely catching himself on the corner of the dining table as one of his legs gave out. But rather than stopping to garner his strength, he took her by the hand and led her across the room and toward the stairs. He didn't guide her up, and instead pulled her into a room beneath the stairs with four beds, two on each side of the room, with small, rectangular tables between each set.

"For your patients," he explained. "I thought if you were to have house visits, you might need somewhere for them to stay." He patted one of the tables. "For supplies. I don't know what you need, but I thought it would be useful."

Her eyes smarted at his thoughtfulness, and her words fled her as he pulled her up the winding staircase leading to the next level instead of waiting for her response.

Curiosity probed her in the side when he skipped a door on their right and continued up the winding stairs until they reached a door preventing them from ascending any higher. He opened it to reveal four bunk beds, making eight beds in total, with adorable hand-woven bedspreads and a chest filled with toys. Several dolls lay across two of the beds, and a walk-in closet rested against the curve of the tree.

"Nyana insisted on this room," he explained, though he bashfully covered his face with his hand before he dropped it to reveal the flush in his cheeks. "I told her I didn't know if children were in our future. I'm not exactly in my twenties anymore and you have a good career. But she claimed it could be used as a guest room when they came to visit."

Emotion knotted in her throat as she stepped inside and ran her fingers over one of the finely crafted beds. "Do you want children?" she finally asked hoarsely. "Well, aside from the ones you already have."

She was still young enough to bear them.

"Whatever you decide, I am happy to go along with it."

She continued trailing her fingers along a bed, the mattress covered by a green and pink knitted blanket. "I admit I never gave it much thought. I never imagined I'd find myself married, let alone have a child."

But the thought of caring for a child or two warmed her heart. Emeric was so supportive of her career, that she was certain he would step up to be the main caretaker while she focused on her ambitions.

Taking her hand, he led her back to the top of the staircase and sighed dramatically. "Ugh. Stairs."

Laughter burst out of her, and she briefly reached out with her magic to assess the status of his legs. His muscles were much stronger than even a few days ago, but she knew standing all day for their intimate ceremony and the celebrations afterward had taken a toll on his strength.

Still, he guided her halfway down the staircase until they stood in front of the previous closed door. It opened up into a large room with a bed, fireplace, armoires, and more. A canopy of flowering vines and branches created a beautiful addition to the room. White flower petals lay strewn across the ground and the bed. And blue crystal sconces lit up the room, creating a magnificent yet cozy atmosphere.

"I love it," she breathed. "All of it. This is the perfect home. I'm so happy to share it with you, Em."

He released a sigh of pure relief. "I've been so nervous you might hate it."

"Never. It's more than I could have ever hoped for."

She threw her arms around his neck and pulled him into a kiss. But that kiss turned into two, which turned into three, until the fire of passion ignited in her belly. However, she broke away with heavy breaths.

"I should let you rest."

"I'm steady," he reassured, trailing the back of his fingers against her cheek. "I'm steady."

And then a vine shot out and pulled her abruptly against him until he devoured her lips in a hungry kiss filled with passion and love.

"You are my healing angel," he murmured against her neck. "I'm looking forward to spending the rest of my life with you."

She twisted his hair around her finger and kissed the corner of his mouth. "It will be an unforgettable adventure."

ABOUT THE AUTHOR

Sydney Winward is an award-winning fantasy and paranormal romance author who dabbles in the occasional historical fiction. She loves building complex worlds filled with magic, strong characters, and emotional stories that can make you laugh and cry.

Sydney is the author of the Sunlight and Shadows Series and the best-selling Bloodborn Series, and when she's not writing, she's reading, thinking about stories, or going on adventures with her children. She lives in Utah with her husband and three amazing kids.

www.sydneywinward.com

www.ingramcontent.com/pod-product-compliance
Lightning Source LLC
Chambersburg PA
CBHW030817200726
48288CB00004B/1276